"Is This Helping?" Nate Asked.

Eve nodded as Nate began a gentle kneading motion down her cramped leg. Absently she cupped both hands around her knee and rubbed the tenderness there. *Why didn't he remember her?* she wondered silently. *Did their night together mean so little to him?*

Casually he said, "I noticed you coming out of that cottage as you started your run. Do you live around here permanently, or are you just vacationing?"

"Vacationing," Eve replied faintly. She couldn't believe that he still didn't know who she was. She intended to add a cutting comment when she looked into his eyes. Her words died in her throat when Nate glanced at her slender left hand.

"Hmm. No ring." A quick smile lit his face, and his eyes were warm and smoky—and utterly devoid of recognition!

Dear Reader:

Six down, six to go... It's July, and I hope you've been enjoying our "Year of the Man." From January to December, 1989 is a twelve-month extravaganza at Silhouette Desire. We're spotlighting one book each month with special cover treatment as a tribute to the Silhouette Desire hero—our *Man of the Month*!

Created by your favorite authors, these men are utterly irresistible. One of Lass Small's Lambert sisters gets a very special man in July. *Man of the Month* Graham Rawlins may start as the *Odd Man Out*, but that doesn't last long....

And Mr. August, Joyce Thies's *Mountain Man* thinks he's conquered it all by facing Alaska, America's last frontier—but he hasn't met his mail-order bride yet!

Yours,

Isabel Swift
Senior Editor & Editorial Coordinator

ASHLEY SUMMERS
Eternally Eve

Silhouette Desire

Published by Silhouette Books New York

America's Publisher of Contemporary Romance

SILHOUETTE BOOKS
300 East 42nd St., New York, N.Y. 10017

ISBN: 0-373-05509-9

First Silhouette Books printing July 1989

Printed in the U.S.A.

Books by Ashley Summers

Silhouette Romance

Season Enchantment #197
A Private Eden #223

Silhouette Desire

Fires of Memory #36
The Marrying Kind #95
Juliet #291
Heart's Delight #374
Eternally Eve #509

ASHLEY SUMMERS

is an incurable romantic. Her busy life revolves around the man she married thirty years ago, her three children and her handsome grandson, Eric. Formerly the owner and operator of a landscaping firm, she still enjoys maintaining her large yard. Other hobbies include biking, aerobics, reading and traveling.

Prologue

His eyelids twitched. The long body that lay between starchy white sheets stirred almost imperceptibly. His mind, although trapped in confusion, protested those sheets. *He* didn't sleep on scratchy, crackly sheets. *His* bed linens were satin.

The absurdity of his indignancy lighted a spark of humor in some distant realm of his being. Then it winked out, leaving him adrift again on his dark sea.

Perplexed and annoyed, he tried to lift his lashes. But they were glued to his cheeks. He turned his struggle inward, to the murk that enwrapped his senses. *Where am I?* The urgent question shredded the mists but gave him no immediate answers. Muted noises filtered through from somewhere: rustling skirts, running water, murmuring voices.

Sensations rushed in. Sunlight slanted across his face. His entire body was stiff and sore. It burned and stung in a dozen different places. He flexed his right arm, and the movement generated pain. His head ached abominably.

Someone was talking too loudly, and he ordered them to stop it. They laughed delightedly.

When he next drew conscious breath, the scent of disinfectant assaulted his nostrils. To his immense relief, his eyes opened. Blurred impressions swamped him. Dusk-shrouded windows and twinkling city lights. What city? he wondered. Los Angeles, of course; that's where he lived. What day was it? April tenth. Satisfied, he examined his surroundings.

White walls, white tile floors, a hospital bed! Why was he in a hospital bed? Was he sick? He discovered a cast on his right arm. Why? When? How? Lord have mercy, did he still have all his faculties? Was his body still functioning, his legs still attached, his manhood intact?

The touch of cool fingers on his wrist halted his mental explorations. A nurse had materialized beside him. Her face was vaguely familiar. She called him Nate, and he wondered if that was his name. Behind her came a Lincolnesque man, a doctor in a flapping white coat. He poked and prodded, checked pupils and reflexes and said, "Good, good."

The doctor's voice kept floating away from Nate, like a wind that came and went, leaving him comforted without quite realizing why. He stopped trying to resist the irresistible and let his mind close down again....

He awoke feeling stronger and much more clearheaded. With painstaking care he gathered fragments of memory and shaped them into fact. He knew he had been injured and that he was still in functioning good order, relatively speaking. He knew his injuries consisted of a severe concussion, cracked ribs, a broken arm and dislocated shoulder. And that was all he knew.

The thought engendered surprise and then quick defensive denial. He'd had some sort of accident he didn't remember. He must have been brought to the emergency room last night, apparently unconscious, since he didn't remember that, either.

He looked down the long powerful body that had served him well for twenty-seven years. His IV had been disconnected; his arm was now folded across his chest. Automatically he glanced at his watch and found instead a plastic bracelet imprinted with his full name—Nathaniel Wright. That frail spark of humor resurfaced. *Well, at least I won't forget who I am.*

Footsteps snagged his attention. Slowly, blinking the thick sable lashes that fringed his gray eyes, he turned his head toward the other side of the bed and the man who sat slumped in an armchair. "Patrick? What time is it?"

His husky baritone voice had the effect of a cattle prod on Patrick Taggart, who shot to his feet and grasped his friend's free hand with a barely suppressed roar. "Nearly midnight. It's about time you showed some signs of life! Dammit, how do you feel?" he demanded, scowling ferociously. "Are you hurting anywhere? Do you want a nurse or something?"

"No, I don't want a nurse of something!" Scowling back, Nate gripped the long tanned fingers as hard as he could before letting go. "What I want is to know what the devil happened to me. Did I have an accident? I must have, but how could I? I went straight to bed after you and Bob left."

"After Bob and I left?" Patrick's eyebrows knit into a puzzled frown. "Left where? When?"

Irritation sharpened Nate's voice. This was a hell of a time to play games. "My apartment, Patrick, last night."

"Last night," Patrick echoed, clearly baffled. "Nate, I haven't been to your apartment in over a week."

"A week?" Incredulous, and just as baffled, Nate stared at him. "You mean I've been unconscious for a week? Why? Good God, Pat, what's wrong with me?"

"Hey, take it easy, man. Nothing's wrong with you! At least nothing permanent. I spoke with the doctor, and he said you'd be fully recovered in no time. But the rest of your question…" Patrick shook his curly black head. "I can answer the when and how. You had dinner and drinks at Angelo's last night and fell down the stairs and knocked yourself out, among other things." He forced a chuckle. "Scared Angelo half to death! Me, too, when he called to say what hospital you were in."

Sobering, Patrick continued, "I know you're pretty banged up, but all things considered, I'd say you were lucky, old friend. Damn lucky, in fact. Those were stone steps beneath that carpet."

His gruff tone gentled. "Last night was Tuesday, Nate. This is Wednesday. You've been out for twenty-four hours now."

"Twenty-four hours? But you said it's been a week since…" Nate paused, drew a long breath and slowly released it. His deepening angst constricted his chest. "I don't understand," he said on a calmer note.

"Don't feel alone, buddy. Neither do I." Patrick dropped his wiry frame back into the chair. The shadowed eyes he looked into were confused. "What's the last thing you remember?"

"I told you—you and Bob coming over to watch the ball game Monday night."

"My God!" Patrick exclaimed softly. "Nate, that was over a week ago."

"No, now that just can't be, Pat," Nate insisted angrily. "I got up the next morning and I..." He shuddered and shut his eyes as his stomach lurched, a sickening sensation much like the downside of a roller-coaster ride. Desperately he strained to recall what he'd done that Tuesday morning. Or Wednesday morning, for that matter. Thursday and Friday, the weekend...nothing. The time he sought to reconstruct was a total blank.

Defeated, he requested dully, "So tell me, what *did* I do Tuesday morning? Last Tuesday, I mean." He touched the bandage angling down one cheek. "It's pretty apparent what I did this Tuesday."

"You did what you usually do—went to the office, played racquetball that evening, had a few drinks around the pool and went to bed. Routine."

Nate nodded. He remembered none of it. But Patrick would know. They worked for the same firm, lived in the same apartment complex. "And the rest of the week? Also routine?"

"Yes. Up until Friday, that is."

"What happened Friday?" Nate asked sharply.

"You went to Vegas. Left Friday evening, returned Sunday afternoon," came Patrick's laconic response. Nate knew that the more upset his friend was, the less he said.

Las Vegas! Nate shut his eyes tightly and explored the hidden channels of his memory, only to come up against a blank wall. But the wall wasn't thick enough to keep emotions from seeping through. *Las Vegas!* Something had happened there, something wrenching enough and poignant enough to squeeze his heart and bring tears to his eyes. But what?

Skepticism gnawed at his small scrap of certainty. Feeling overwhelmed, he gave a strangled laugh. "Funny, huh? The first vacation I've taken in years, and I don't even remember it."

"Yeah, funny."

Studiedly calm, Nate put a name to it. "Amnesia?"

"That would be my guess. Maybe it's just temporary."

"And maybe it's not," Nate countered, feeling combative. "Maybe it's permanent."

"Maybe," Patrick conceded quietly. "Either way, you'll know when the doctor comes back in the morning."

"Maybe." The repetitious word snapped the simmering tension as both men responded to it.

"Sometimes it's a wait-and-see situation," Nate went on distractedly. His attempt to accept his own diagnosis was turning into a mental wrestling match.

Amnesia. He couldn't even relate to the word. It just wasn't *real.* People in books got amnesia, spies with deadly secrets, adventurous heroines and swashbuckling heroes. None of those descriptions fit a man who not only didn't know how to swashbuckle, but whose tongue was prone to tangle whenever he found himself in the company of unattached, aggressively interested women.

So okay, Nate, he chided himself. Putting aside your artful way with the ladies, how else can you account for this twilight zone you've stumbled into? You can't! You can't cope with it, either. But you're double-blasted well going to have to.

With a wry half smile, Nate conceded his dilemma. He needed to do some straight thinking, but he felt so addled he couldn't even focus. The intrusion of another nurse was almost comic relief.

She was trim, graceful and old enough to be his mother, but the smile she gave her patient was something less than maternal. Nate, with his big gray eyes and irregular features, was an uncommonly good-looking man. A fingertip-deep dimple tempered his stubborn chin. His hair had the rich dark sheen of chestnuts, and not even a top sheet and blanket could obscure the clean masculine lines of his six-foot frame.

Nate saw Patrick grin as yet another attractive female popped in to check on things.

"Popular patient," he observed when the room emptied.

"Humph." Without thinking, Nate shifted position and winced as pain speared his rib cage. "Ouch! Damn things *hurt*."

"You should have taken that shot."

"I hate shots." He rubbed his bristly chin, a tired gesture.

Patrick slipped into his loafers. "Want me to go?"

"No, not yet." Meeting the appraising blue gaze, Nate quipped weakly, "I need an anchor while I'm wandering through this twilight zone."

"Good name for it," Patrick approved.

Nate smiled one-sidedly and turned his face to the wall. Coping time, he admonished himself. Closing his eyes, he focused all his energy on retrieving the immediate past.

The only result was a crackling in his ears. There was simply nothing between Monday night's ball game and now. Incredible! He shivered. A whole week of his life, lost, maybe forever. Three days in Vegas, a complete mystery. And a disturbing one.

But why? he wondered again. *Had* something happened there? Something that had left a residue of soft aching sadness and a gnawing sense of deprivation, as if some sweet bright warmth had gone out of his life?

Patrick's voice was a welcome interruption to his perplexing thoughts. "Nate, I've notified everyone you'd want to know about your accident—" he hesitated "—but I didn't call Barbara. Do you want me to?"

"Hell no, I don't want you calling Barbara!"

Chagrined at his explosive response, Nate smiled in wry apology. Barbara was his ex-wife. And probably the source of all these feelings whirling around inside him, he thought with a derisive snort for his embarrassingly romantic fancies about a common Vegas weekend. What he felt was all too easily explained. He had just come through a painful divorce from the woman he had loved deeply, and he was still reeling from the punches.

Barbara's remarriage two short weeks after their own became a statistic was another devastating blow. On top of everything else, he felt like a fool. His whole world had revolved around the gold band he'd put on her finger. Not once had he considered stepping outside its boundaries. But she had, and did.

In retrospect, perhaps that's what had hurt most, Nate mused, remembering the gut-wrenching experience of being forced to stand helplessly by while all his cherished illusions shattered on reality's stony ground. He had always believed that for every man and woman there was a special someone to give meaning to the word *forever*. Well, he'd been proven wrong, he concluded with a savage twist of anger that it should be so.

Oh, for God's sake, let it *go*, Nate! he admonished himself. But as usual, he was wasting his energy. The vicious combination of rejection and betrayal was as hard on a man's ego as it was on his heart.

Seeking a less unsettling line of thought, he broke the silence with a musing, "It'll be tough going back to work when you can't remember what you said or did the week before."

"I imagine it will," Patrick agreed mildly.

Nate sighed. He was a computer expert who had always loved his work, but the prospect of resuming his everyday routine depressed him. The thought of returning to the sleek monochrome apartment that had marked his new status as a "divinely eligible bachelor"—whatever that was—made him feel even worse. Suddenly he wanted, quite desperately, to walk out on it all.

He could buy a yacht, stock it with champagne and pretty ladies and sail wherever the south wind blew him, he thought longingly. He smiled wryly. Oh, come on, Nate, he gibed at his rock-solid self, you're not the playboy type.

Eyeing Pat's weary face, he faked a yawn and said, "Go on home, Pat. I'll be all right."

"You sure?"

"I'm sure," Nate lied. He wasn't sure of anything anymore, except his future plans. He wasn't sailing off to live a vagabond's life, but he was pulling up stakes as soon as he was back on his feet. He felt a sudden insane urge just to get up and go.

There was something out there beyond the darkness, something he had to find. . . .

Alone and lonely in the shadowed room, Nate was easy prey for the fantasies of a needful heart. At that moment the wanting in him was nearly intolerable. He needed to love and be loved—be wanted and loved so much he'd never have cause to wonder, never again feel the corrosive acid of self-doubt and uncertainty gnawing at his guts. God, how he wanted it!

The force of his raw inner cry infuriated him. Even if by some miracle he was attracted to another woman, he'd have to back away. He knew how deep his wounds went. It would take a long time to dissolve the cynicism that had, already, begun to cover them like protective scabs. Regaining the ability to trust again, to open himself up to the emotional intimacies of a relationship, might take forever.

"Just because you're all fouled up is no reason to foul up someone else's life," he advised himself.

He laughed harshly. Such nobility, Nate! he thought. But something deep down inside wasn't laughing.

He was cold and sleepy again. Drawing the sheet up to his chin, Nate lay awake for a moment longer, wondering, idly, intensely, as he suspected he would for years to come: what *did* happen in Vegas?

One

Eve was sitting on the deck eating cherries, when she saw him coming down the beach. The juice of the succulent fruit she had lifted to her mouth stained her bottom lip dark red. Eve wasn't aware of it. She wasn't aware of anything but the man who came toward her with the high-powered grace of a mountain puma.

Her tongue flicked over the tart-sweet wetness of her lips as she watched him. He was looking toward the sea, his profile a sharply etched silhouette of sculpted bone and muscle beneath burnished skin. Long bare legs and well-muscled arms emerged from the white jogging shorts and sleeveless T-shirt that clung to his decidedly masculine frame.

An old and all-too-familiar pain tightened Eve's throat. She swallowed so hard it hurt even worse. It was exasperating that the sight of a certain tall, dark stranger could still quicken her pulses. Senselessly, as it always turned out. First, because it was never him, and second, because she had no reason to want it to be, not anymore.

Studiously, she turned her attention to the task of wiping her mouth and fingers. The late afternoon breeze was getting chilly, and she was poorly dressed for it, having just completed her own run. A hot shower would feel good, and she still had to wash her hair. She and her cousin, Mary Jo, were dining out tonight.

She put the rest of her cherries back into the basket, intending to go inside. But the man she still watched from the corner of her eye was now close enough to see clearly even without her glasses. She hesitated a moment longer, impatient with herself, knowing she was waiting for him to turn his head. Then he did, and she forgot her impatience. She even forgot how to breathe.

The shock was electric, a fiery bolt shot through her body with paralyzing force. It was him. It really was him!

He lifted a hand in greeting as he passed by. Like a marionette, she raised her own hand.

Eve made no attempt to call out to him. It was all she could do to cope with her reaction to his sudden appearance. Joy and excitement ran riot with stunned surprise, and her mind refused to work. When it did, scraps of thought and memories spun off on random courses like whirling dust devils.

His name was Nathaniel Wright. "But you can call me Nate," he had said once upon a starry midnight. And she had. Called him Nate, called him darling, called him love. Called him bastard....

Feeling a need to hang on to something, she clasped her fingers together so tightly they matched the ache that pulsed somewhere deep inside her. Nate. Here. At the same time she was, on the very same section of New Hampshire's beautiful coast. Why? Because of her?

Nonsense! she rebuked herself with a sharpness that quieted her buzzing mind somewhat. It had been nearly five years since their brief affair, with no further contact whatsoever. It wasn't likely that he'd decided to look her up after all this time.

A coincidence, that's all. Just a coincidence.

Her hunched shoulders straightened with a jerk as a question emerged from the functioning part of her mind. Why, when he saw her, hadn't *he* called out to *her*? For that matter, why had he looked at her with nothing more than masculine appreciation?

Unraveling her fingers, she forced herself to relax. Now don't get paranoid, Elizabeth Eve, she chided herself. He didn't see you clearly, that's all. The distance—and the sun was in your face.

A mixture of anxiety and self-annoyance darkened her violet eyes. What had she expected to see when he'd looked at her? Recognition, of course. But nothing else, surely. She'd have to be a fool to think that a weekend fling was in any way special to a man like Nathaniel Wright. Successful. Good-looking. Single. Or was, at the time. He'd probably need a computer just to keep track of his conquests, she concluded with a twist of her lips.

She wondered if he was still single and, angrily, why it should matter. Feeling vulnerable, she averted her eyes. But the gleam of September sunlight on tousled sable hair effortlessly recaptured her gaze. Hair that curled at his nape and sometimes tasted damp and salty, she remembered.

As she watched his pleasing form, memories came at her from all directions. Most were quickly blocked, but a few managed to break through.

Nate, the man. He'd been quiet, courteous, subtly aloof. He'd had the deepest, most infectious laugh she'd ever heard, the sexiest eyes she'd ever seen. Gray with just a hint of blue, like wood smoke rising in a clear winter sky; sometimes they'd been dark and shadowed.

Nate, the lover. Demanding. Taking. Giving. Deliciously rough and tender. Addictive magic.

The unwelcome spate of recall was disquieting. But what threw Eve's mind into renewed turmoil was the unnerving choice thrust upon her with head-spinning swiftness: to meet him or not. Nate had reached the turn-around point and was edging back toward the cottage with casual male intent. He was smiling and she knew that smile. It flashed through her in a sensation so hot and deep she shivered.

Maybe she ought to avoid him, Eve thought uneasily. Meeting him was so risky, and she could go hide inside the cottage, pretend she didn't know him . . . She snorted. Even had it been

possible to escape those sharp gray eyes, which she doubted, her
pride would never permit such a thing. Besides, she was dying
to meet him, if for no other reason than to prove that she was
a mature woman now, quite capable of handling past affairs
with aplomb. I'm someone far different than that silly little
romantic who set myself up for a fall, she thought with a twinge
of sadness for the loss of those lovely youthful illusions.

Granted, her quick decision was a little frightening. But she
was burning with curiosity about the man who had so radi-
cally changed her life, and it all added up to an irresistible
challenge.

So why fight it? What harm could a brief encounter do? She
was the one in control now.

An ironic smile curved Eve's lush mouth as she acknowledged the reason for the nerves fluttering in her stomach. She
wasn't merely afraid—she was scared to death.

The admission straightened her slim back and raised the
point of her chin in proud defiance. This was hardly the time
to start doubting herself. Nate was nearly upon her. A distracting thought brought her to her feet. She couldn't meet him
here! Mary Jo could come in at any second and start flinging
all manner of questions around.

Smoothing her pink shorts, Eve drew a deep breath. A moment later she was down the steps and running along the water's edge toward the huge granite boulder some fifty feet
ahead.

Nate was still behind her. Though Eve set herself a swift
pace, she knew her rapid heartbeat wasn't caused by running.
A slim, finely fashioned woman, she moved with the resilient
grace of the dancer she had once been. Ordinarily a sprint
would have barely elevated her pulse rate. But the long powerful legs carrying him over the sand were rapidly closing the
distance between them. She sensed his assessing male gaze and
felt the hot thrill of awareness as surely as if he'd touched her.

Not ready to face him, Eve lengthened her stride and forged
ahead at an erratic pace, a thoughtless act that resulted in a
twist of pain down the back of her leg. Giving a soft cry, she
crumpled onto the sand.

Instantly he was kneeling beside her, his hands pushing hers away to grasp the shapely calf she clutched. "What happened?" he asked sharply.

Not trusting herself to speak, Eve kept her attention on her leg. Annoyance at her carelessness collided with the tingling pleasure produced by his touch. She couldn't even think straight, much less confront those gray eyes.

When she did reply, her voice was so high and thin even she didn't recognize it. "I don't know. A muscle spasm, I guess."

"Yes, I can feel some tightness here.... Hold still," he commanded when she dared move. Numbly she watched the long fingers sliding up her leg, squeezing her soft flesh, inducing exquisite little bursts of pain to mingle with the warmth of each quick release. "Is this helping?"

She nodded, her throat clogging up again as he began a gentle kneading motion back down her quivering limb. Absently she cupped both hands around her knee and rubbed the tenderness there. When her fingers brushed his, she felt a flash of something very similar to static electricity.

He must have felt it, too, for his hands stilled.

Casually, he said, "I noticed you coming out of that cottage. Do you live here year-round, or are you just vacationing?"

Bending lower to examine the tiny scratch on her leg, Eve inhaled deeply. You ninny, he hasn't really seen you yet! she derided the needling hurt inflicted by his query.

"Vacationing."

"So am I, although I do own a cottage here. I'll be here for several more weeks. How long are you staying?"

"I—I haven't decided yet." Swallowing to bring her voice back down to its naturally soft fluted tones, Eve gave a quick laugh. "This is only my second day, so I'm not sure yet how I'll like it here."

Abruptly she looked up at him, intending to say, "Hi, Nate, long time no see," or some such inanity. But the words died in her throat as Nate glanced first at her face, then at the slender hand that had drifted to the sand like a fallen leaf.

"Hmm. No ring," he commented, that quick smile lighting his face. "Maybe I can help you decide. Nate Wright," he said. "Entirely at your service, ma'am."

His eyes were warm, smoky and utterly devoid of any sign of recognition!

Eve's heart skipped a violent beat as a shock wave hit and then rolled over her. Something tore inside. She gasped, trying desperately not to betray herself.

Anger sliced through her, freezing her emotions. Coolly she met his quizzical regard.

"Eve Sheridan. Not at your service, however," she snapped. "But thank you. My leg feels fine now."

"My pleasure, Eve," he said softly.

The intensity of his gaze brought Eve's lashes down in swift defense. His compelling gray eyes seemed to strip away barriers and pry into private places, as if to uncover the secret locked within.

Unable to think of anything to say, she pulled the cloth ring from her ponytail, thrilling to his swift intake of breath as the smooth golden mass fell fluidly around her face and shoulders. Shaking it back, she looked him square in the eye. Not a flicker of recognition! She set her mouth and held the look challengingly.

It was a challenge Nate Wright delighted in taking. This provocative woman filled his body with radiant good feelings and his mind with intriguing confusions. A seductive combination, he thought as warmth suffused him. His gaze flowed over her set features and moved downward to rest on her small outthrust breasts, the delectable curve of hips and those long elegant legs.

Meeting her eyes again was nearly his undoing. They were narrowed warningly, and he felt a feather of absurdly tender laughter tickle his throat. She was enchanting!

"I'd still like a try at convincing you to stay around for a while, starting tonight with some good food and dancing," he went on lightly. He picked up her hand and frowned at the hard little calluses on her palm. "What are these from?"

"Gardening." Too engrossed in his thumb sliding slowly back and forth across her palm to respond to his invitation, Eve retrieved her hand, then nervously tucked a wing of hair behind one ear. He still hadn't taken his eyes off her. Tilting her head, she subjected him to the same intense scrutiny.

What she saw both pleased and disturbed her. There wasn't a hint of softness in the hard line of his jaw, no weakness to be found in his firm mouth or clefted chin. He radiated the uncompromising surety of a man who knew and liked himself.

His expression bemused, he smoothed the tuft of hair that curled up to form a cowlick at the back of his head, a painfully familiar gesture to Eve. She had loved to smooth it for him, tame it into submission.

Unconsciously, her lips parted in a secretive smile. *She'd been trying to tame that beguiling little cowlick for years now.*

Her mouth tightened as she caught his eye. Looking rueful, Nate murmured, "Pardon my staring, but you're an incredibly attractive woman, Eve Sheridan. Fascinating, in fact. Absolutely fascinating."

Tensing, Eve glanced away. Once her craving for his approval would have enslaved her, made of her a spineless creature willing to do anything to be the recipient of that slow, bone-melting smile. But no more, she assured herself. Such dangerous weaknesses had long since been conquered.

"Thank you," she said stiffly.

"You're welcome," came his slightly amused response.

Her chin whipped up. Was he laughing at her, perhaps finding her cautious manner with him an entertainment for his ego? "You are, too," she tossed out. "Attractive, I mean."

"Thank you," he said gravely. Straightening, he pulled off his T-shirt and wiped his damp brow, an unthinking act that sent a thrill of alarm spidering down her spine. Somehow—and looking at him it seemed downright impossible—she had forgotten just how alluring Nathaniel Wright could be to a woman. A sprinkling of dark curls adorned his chest. His broad shoulders and back tapered to a pleasingly trim waist. He was well muscled, but not massively so. Instead, the sinewy strength rippling beneath his golden skin had the tightly coiled power of a Thoroughbred.

Realizing she was staring as if she'd never seen a naked chest before, Eve ignored the heat in her cheeks and continued crisply, "You're welcome. Well, now that we've got that set- tled, I think I'll go exercise this leg before it stiffens up on me. Goodbye, Nate. It was nice meeting you."

A hand caught her arm. Nate laughed easily, seemingly un- bothered at her careless dismissal, but there was no mistaking the expression flaring in his eyes. Still a bit of the macho male, Eve thought with vexing ambivalence. She liked the masculine assurance he exuded almost as much as she resented it.

She frowned.

"Well, Eve, I can't just let you up and walk away!" he pro- tested, his rich baritone laced with laughter. "We haven't de- cided where we'll have dinner tonight, or what time, for that matter."

Her violet eyes, sparkling like sunlight on ice, stared into his. "Don't presume, Nate."

"I wouldn't dare." His laughter died. "I just wanted to spend the evening together, and I hoped the feeling was mu- tual."

Eve hesitated. The feeling *was* mutual—and that was the hell of it.

He took a strand of her hair and let it run through his fin- gers. "It doesn't really matter what we do. I simply would like, very much, and for reasons I can't explain but which feel very good, to spend the entire evening just being with you. We can just sit here in the sand and try to outstare each other, for all I care."

Eve felt color retinting her cheeks. Damn him! His husky words had tangled up her breathing apparatus again.

"Hey." Nate touched her nose. "Are we on for dinner or not?"

"I trust you're not married or otherwise committed?"

"Neither married nor committed," Nate answered with a mildness his tight smile belied. "If I were, I wouldn't be doing this." He leaned back on his hands and crossed his ankles. "You said you were vacationing. Where are you from?"

"Here. That is, New Hampshire. I live in Concord."

"Alone?"

"No, with my—my housekeeper," she stammered, taken aback by his sharpness. "I'd better get on back to the cottage."

Lazily Nate uncoiled to his full height and pulled her up beside him. "Tonight's very casual, a luau at the Wagners', just up the hill from you. Are you big on pit-cooked food and torchlight dancing?"

"I don't know...." Shaken by his nearness and the differing desires he aroused, Eve licked her dry lips. You're the one in control here, she reminded herself with gritty determination. And all the while her mind was painting pictures as starkly physical as the line of hair arrowing down his lean midriff. "Since I've never tried that particular combination before," she ended with a touch of asperity.

"I think you'll like it." He paused, smiling that wry, delicious, damnable male smile that wreaked havoc with her sensible intent. "Always assuming, of course, that you do want to go."

"It sounds lovely. But I have other plans for tonight," she explained, savoring the bittersweet satisfaction of watching his expression change. She knew he was hurt, because she'd seen that look so often. Tough, she thought coldly. Her lips curved into a gracious smile. "But thank you, Nate."

She turned and ran back down the beach, leaving him standing there with a baffled look on his face.

Closing the cottage door behind her was similar to surfacing from a deep dive. Eve leaned against the living room wall and balled her hands into fists. Both her pride and ego had suffered enormous blows from Nate's lapse of memory, she admitted. But she could and would handle it sensibly. Especially when she'd calmed down a bit.

Unable to resist one last look at him, she turned to the window and pulled aside the creamy muslin draperies to see nothing but a sandpiper, the ocean and a huge granite boulder. He had vanished as easily as a mirage.

As he had once before. The feelings that flared from that undisciplined thought made her lean against the wall again. It was jolting to realize he could be dangerous in a way she hadn't expected after all this time.

He's just a man, she told herself sternly.

But he wasn't just a man.

She looked into the mirror hanging on the opposite wall, and frowned at the haunting sadness that darkened the violet eyes staring back at her. Enough thinking, she sternly decided. What she needed right now was therapeutic action. Kicking off her shoes, she eased into one of her aerobic stretch-and-tone routines, then headed for the bathroom.

A long hot shower and vigorous shampoo were proven restoratives. Feeling cleansed of her jittery tension, she sat down on the cushioned window seat in her bedroom to deal with the painful issue she'd evaded earlier.

Nate didn't remember her.

Why didn't he remember? How could he not! Eve clenched her jaw while the silent inner cry ran its twisting course. The question had battered her mind all during their encounter and would continue to do so, she suspected, regardless of how she answered it. And the only answer she could come up with offhand was so elemental it stung like a nest of maddened hornets. Their weekend together simply hadn't been memorable.

Eve tried to downplay her hurt with ironic humor. At least she now knew what their affair had meant to him. But her pride couldn't accept that stark answer. There *had* to be other reasons! Leaving the window seat, she went to her mirror and began brushing her damp hair while she sought them out.

There was the drastic change in her appearance to consider. In fact, she was a totally different person from that small-town golden girl who had headed to Vegas with a dazzling dream, only to end up a brassy redhead waiting tables in a friend's small dinner club. But on that fateful night, she'd gotten a chance to dance in the chorus line and had caught Nate's attention....

The brush went through her hair in quick hard strokes as Eve directed her mind back to the subject. With her face scrubbed of its heavy makeup and her hair restored to its original color, the image in her mirror was a far cry from her anemic imitation of a glamorous show girl.

That rationale didn't set well with her, either—surely the man had seen through the dyed hair and heavy makeup—but it was the best she could do. Of course, she was as tough as nails now....

Tossing down her brush, Eve scrutinized her face, as if she'd never seen it before. That tender mouth, those pansy-purple eyes. "About as tough as a soft-shelled crab," she said with a sigh. "Hi, Mary Jo!" she caroled, looking up with a warm smile as a petite woman with dark eyes and a riot of short black curls slumped into the room.

Mary Jo's posture was not indicative of her mood. She'd had a great day, she announced, returning Eve's hug, and she couldn't wait to get to the party.

"Party?" Eve echoed. "What party? You said we were going out to dinner."

"We are. It's a dinner party. A luau at the Wagners'. You'll love it," Mary Jo stated, and rushed back out of the room bewailing her wind-ravaged appearance.

"So I've been told," Eve muttered. Trying to ignore the hollow feeling pitting her stomach, she dressed in a strapless print jumpsuit and matching jacket, then finished brushing her hair. The autumn-gold mass flowed to her waist, fine and utterly straight, the same absurd extravagance that had tested her childhood mettle. Now, however, rather than the detested scalp-pinching braids, she wore it parted at the side, with an expertly layered wing curving deeply over one eyebrow.

Shades of apricot and taupe eye shadow and a sunny coral lipstick sufficed for makeup. Slipping on her low-heeled pumps, she went outside to the deck to wait.

The warm weather that enwrapped the coast, so rare for this time of year, was a delight to the senses. Seabirds called in the deepening dark, and the last of summer's roses spilled their perfume over rock-garden walls. Fixing her gaze on the pink-and-gold ruffle of sunlight that separated the merging gray of horizon and sea, she leaned pensively against the rail.

Such dusky beauty made her feel soft and vulnerable, and her nervous system was still a little haywire from her encounter with Nate. So why on earth, she demanded of herself, was she going to the same party? *Because it's as irresistible as a box of chocolates, that's why. And you, Elizabeth Eve,* she con-

cluded dryly, tasting again the bittersweet flavor of refusing
him, *are a closet chocoholic*.

When Mary Jo joined her, Eve quickly donned an air of
careless poise perfected by years of use. Only the fast-beating
pulse at her throat betrayed her anxiety. Deciding to walk the
short distance, they followed the beach path to a line of flaring torches that led them across a raked-sand yard to an elaborate terrace studded with people, flowers and candlelit tables.

Tall fences and shrubbery sheltered the area from the wind,
and a driftwood fire cast its coppery radiance over the festive
crowd. The atmosphere was sparkling and apparently conta-
gious, for Eve's spirits swiftly soared. Since she had not yet
spied Nate, she drifted toward the next best thing, a long food-
laden table.

But Nate had spied her, and with a surprisingly strong shock
of recognition. Crazy, he thought. He'd only just met the
woman. His breath caught as she shed her jacket and tossed it
on a chair. In the soft firelight she was a golden nymph, the pale
gold silk of flawless skin, the richer, deeper gold of hair, the
patterned gold of her garment. He watched her with a peculiar
delight. He was aware of the excitement pounding in his blood
and quite enjoyed the quickening of every male sense.

The sharpness of his initial response, however, was something else again. He didn't know what to make of it, or even
how to define the feeling she aroused. But they were there.

Irritably Nate dismissed them and let his attention flicker to
the pretty brunette standing beside her. Eve's choice of companion was a lovely relief. Both her turndown and his assumption that she'd done so in favor of another man had gouged his
ego badly. He wondered why she hadn't told him differently.
Feminine games, he supposed. A forthright man, he disliked
games. But this was Eve, and somehow that made all the difference.

With a faint smile at his biased tolerance, he started toward
her, only to stop as if he had run into an invisible wall as her
wandering gaze found him. For the second time today, he
found himself baffled by the conflicting signals she sent out.
Invitingly accessible and coolly untouchable, she presented a
challenge no red-blooded male could resist. Yet he couldn't

detect a hint of the guile that usually accompanied this feminine tactic.

Frustrated at his lack of perception, Nate cocked his head with less than his usual assurance. The appealing face framed by blowing tresses had suddenly assumed a look of pinched wariness.

Then she tipped her head in devastating mimicry, her grin mocking his confusion. Nate's dry laugh mocked himself. His imagination, like his libido, was running wild tonight. Confidently he strode toward her. Color flared along the high planes of her cheeks as their gazes held and a strange soft tenderness moved within him.

"Hello again," he said huskily.

"Hi, Nate. Need a plate?" she asked brightly, reaching for one. She glanced behind him. "No date tonight?"

"Couldn't get one," he murmured.

"I doubt that," she said as dry as dust. "This is my cousin, Mary Jo Sheridan," she hurried on, aided by the nudge in her ribs. "Mary Jo, Nathaniel Wright. We ran into each other on the beach this afternoon."

Curious dark eyes flashed over him from head to toe. Humorously aware of Mary Jo's appraisal, he endured their brief social exchange distractedly at best. Eve's perfume was affecting him like an intimate caress.

Her face was upturned to his. She was tall for a woman, Nate realized dazedly. He was six foot two, and if he bent his head a little, he could kiss the tip of her nose. Reining in his urges, he automatically took the plate she held out. Mary Jo had turned to speak with someone, and for a shimmering moment he was alone with Eve, alone in a crowd that simply flickered out as he drifted into the mysterious depths of wide violet-blue eyes.

She shattered the moment by handing him another plate. "Here, hold mine, too, and I'll serve us both. Chicken or pork?"

"Chicken, please. Breast." The sensuous smile that had taken command of his mouth wrapped itself around her name. "Eve, why didn't you tell me you were coming to this party?"

"Because it was none of your business," she replied sweetly. "Sweet potato?"

"What? Oh, yes, thank you." Nate waited until she had sliced open the roasted tuber and dolloped it with butter before saying, "I'll grant you that, but why did you let me believe you were coming with me? Why didn't you just say no right off?"

"I had my reasons." She slanted him a glance. "For one, you were a little too sure of yourself. Never could abide a presumptuous male," she drawled. "Anything else?"

Nate shook his head, not sure if she was referring to his questions or his plate. It didn't matter; his appetite had vanished along with their privacy. Uninvited and not giving a damn, he followed her to one of the pink-linened tables. Mary Jo joined them, and shortly after that another male clapped Nate on the shoulder with a jolly laugh.

"Well, Nate, trust you to latch on to the two prettiest girls at the party," Patrick Taggart chided.

"And trust you to show up and spoil it all," Nate said bitterly, grasping his friend's hand with open affection. Looking resigned, he introduced Patrick, who promptly scooted in between the two women and explained that he'd be here all weekend.

Eve liked him immediately, an obvious fact Nate noted with good-natured envy. Along with charmingly irregular features and the wee bald spot that crowned his curly dark head, Patrick had the kind of cheerful, breezy personality that virtually eliminated awkwardness.

Eve was at ease with him, something Nate would have given a great deal to say for himself. As the evening passed, she laughed and chattered and even indulged in several of the fast nontouching dances that left him hot and hungry for more, but he sensed the distance she inserted between them.

It perplexed him. *She* perplexed him. He still hadn't mastered the fine art of snappy lines and meaningless patter, and doubted he ever would, but he did know how to treat a lady. Yet, regardless of how softly he spoke or how gentle his manner, there was an elusive startled-doe quality about Eve, as if he were the danger from which she stood poised to run.

Mysteries and secrets. Intriguing, he admitted, letting his hand touch her bare shoulder. The silken muscles beneath his palm promptly rejected his touch, and a glint of anger lighted his gray eyes. He didn't need this. As if to support his thought, a statuesque brunette in supple red leather sauntered by with a sultry smile. Nate expelled an exasperated breath. What he needed and what he wanted seemed miles apart tonight.

In the next instant he reversed his thinking as the music turned soft and slow. Lightly he touched a golden tress. "Would you like to try that?"

"No, thank you," Eve added automatically. She wasn't interested in dancing; the strain of her evening had hit her and just scraping up a smile to soften her refusal required enormous effort. Nor did she care to follow Mary Jo and Patrick's example and take a walk on the beach, another of Nate's suggestions that taxed her badly frayed nerves.

All she really wanted, Eve decided dully, was the blessed security of her bed. When Nate offered to drive her home, she accepted without hesitation.

The mercifully short drive was completed in silence, for which Eve was thankful. She meant to get out of the car quickly, but the fingers curling around her wrist stayed her progress.

"Eve, I want to see you again," Nate said in a quiet, deep voice she had never forgotten.

"Oh, Nate." Eve sighed. Her tired brain floundered between caution and desire, between reality and fantasy. "I don't know. Call me tomorrow," she said, and got out of the car with sharp, self-directed impatience. "Nate, you don't have to see me to the door," she protested as he swung around the car to meet her.

"Of course I'll see you to the door. I'm a gentleman," Nate said in light rebuke.

He escorted her to the moon-shadowed porch with a hand tucked under her elbow, a courtly gesture, but then, gentlemen did that, she thought, swallowing a hysterical giggle. Gentlemen just didn't remember when or to whom they did that.

Acutely aware of his nearness, she unlocked the door and opened it. "I appreciate the ride home, Nate. The evening was lovely, thanks to you,'' she said nicely. "I hope you enjoyed it as much as I did.''

"More, I think.'' The big hands settling on her shoulders suspended her breath. "Eve. Lovely, alluring Eve,'' he whispered. Instinctively Eve tipped her face to his. She had to have the kiss he wanted. She had to *know*.

His words had been a husky rasp of desire, yet his lips brushed across hers as if asking permission. Did she give it? She must have, for his hands were suddenly hot on her back, his arms enwrapping her with that odd hint of possessiveness, molding her to the taut length of his body.

Eve's grip on reality fluctuated madly. All evening she had wondered what it would be like to kiss him again, and it was worse than anything she had imagined. His mouth took hers with inflaming hunger, making her taste and feel his desire, making her aware of her womanhood as no other man ever had. She seemed to drink him in, her thirsting lips, her swelling breasts, her swiftly hazing mind. Any thoughts of control were temporarily obliterated by the tempestuous warmth enveloping her entire body.

Lights shining down the narrow road shocked her to her senses. Eve jerked her head aside with a gasp of dismay. God, what had come over her? Her hands were buried in his hair, her body practically glued to his—and all of it was now brightly spotlighted.

"Eve?'' Nate questioned softly.

The flush of shame and self-anger had to burn its relentless way through her before Eve could speak. "Good night, Nate,'' she said quickly, and went inside.

Mary Jo followed just a moment later. "Hope I didn't disrupt anything important out there,'' she murmured, dark eyes dancing.

Eve hung up her jacket while she struggled to regain some composure. "No, you didn't. Patrick bring you home?''

"Yeah, he's a nice guy.'' Mary Jo flopped down on the couch. "How about your friend, the fascinating Mr. Wright? Could he be *Mr. Right* by the remotest chance?'' she inquired with a mischievous grin.

"'Mr. Right.' Oh God, that's ironic, Mary Jo!" Eve said, beginning to laugh with a harsh, strangled sound.

"Evie?" Mary Jo asked uncertainly.

Struggling for control, Eve dragged a hand across her face. "I'm sorry, but it hurts, damn it! I didn't expect it to hurt, I... You want to hear something else ironic, Mary Jo? He didn't recognize me. I spent an entire evening with him and he..."

She gulped for air. "The father of my child didn't recognize me!"

Two

***

Mary Jo leaped the couch in a single bound, her fierce embrace threatening to crush bones. "Oh Eve, I'm sorry, so sorry! I never had a clue." Her voice cracked. "Nathaniel Wright? *He's* the one who left you stranded?"

"He's the one," came Eve's muffled reply.

"And he didn't even recognize you? But why not? And all evening—how you must have felt! That bastard! That scroungy egg-sucking *polecat*!" Mary Jo swore so ferociously that Eve found a weak laugh mingling with her tears.

"Oh, come on, Mary Jo—'egg-sucking polecat'? That's hitting pretty low, don't you think?" she chided, wiping her eyes. "Besides, he didn't have a clue, either."

"I'd like to hit even lower," Mary Jo said grimly. Dashing at her own wet eyes, she hurried to the small bar and slopped some brandy into a glass. "Here, sit down and drink this. Why didn't he have a clue? And how on earth could he not recognize you?"

"Would you like to know how many times I've asked myself that?" Eve inquired with wintry dryness. Obediently she sipped the fiery liquor. "I think, or maybe just hope, that my appearance had something to do with it. When I met him in Vegas, I had red hair and one of those perms with frizzy little curls growing wild all over my head...."

She hesitated, reluctant to expose her scarred pride to possible derision. She had never revealed the details of her affair, just announced the results in the coarse, defensive language used to describe an unwanted pregnancy. She doubted that her present flippancy had fooled Mary Jo, but her cousin respected it for what it was, a valiant means of coping with an intolerable situation.

Eve often had cause to regret the reserve she had wrapped around herself. As girls growing up in North Carolina, she and Mary Jo had shared their hopes, their dreams, their deepest secrets. But although only eight months separated their ages, in experience Eve felt decades older than her blithe-hearted younger cousin. And while their friendship was still as warm and loving as ever, the wonderful habit of sharing had not survived.

Well, Eve decided, if she had been the one to destroy it, she could at least make a stab at resurrecting it. With stoic candor, she continued, "But that wasn't the only reason Nate forgot me, Mary Jo. A one-night stand simply isn't that memorable to a man."

Mary Jo sat down with a thump. "A one-night stand? *You?*"

"That's about what it amounted to, for him, at least. Actually, we had a weekend, but that doesn't alter the facts. I guess in a situation like that, a man doesn't really see the person, only what absorbs his interests. Apparently I made no more impression on him than a masseuse you employ once or twice." Eve's mouth trembled at her stinging choice of words, but she'd learned to be tough on herself. "Attentive and charming, oh yes, but he didn't see *me*. Just an aggregate of feminine parts."

"Elizabeth Eve Sheridan, of all the bull-hockey! You know damn good and well that's not true. No man could look at you and see just *parts*."

Eve's shoulders sagged. She ached to believe that, but hard logic was inarguable, she told herself even while she argued, "I didn't think so while it was happening, and even back then I was a cautious person. Until Nate came along, I'd never broken my rule about dating the club's customers.''

"But he was different," Mary Jo prodded when her cousin fell silent.

"Yes, he was," Eve said with a trace of defiance. "He didn't grab, he didn't make lewd remarks, he didn't even make a pass at me that first night. After dinner we just went to the casino and gambled. Winning or losing didn't seem to matter to him, although he got a kick out of my excitement when I won. Around dawn he took me to my apartment, kissed my nose and left. I thought I must have bored him, but the next night there he was, waiting for me to get off work. I was waitressing, I remember, and he didn't like that. He asked me, real sharp, 'Aren't those trays too heavy for you?' They were, but he's the only one who ever noticed."

Her face softened and a dreamy lilt stole into her voice. "He was twenty-seven then, and he had no idea how old I was. All that makeup, those scanty costumes and the airs I put on... How could he have guessed I was only nineteen? That night we went up to his suite, and he ordered a champagne supper served on the balcony. It was a gorgeous night, hot and still and starry. We talked for hours. He wanted to know everything about me! Then we went inside and we... I slept in his arms all that night. I couldn't get free, not that I wanted to, but every time I stirred, his arms would tighten as if he couldn't bear to let me go."

Mockery edged her low tone. "And why not? We were perfectly attuned to each other, bound together in every way possible. Needless to say, it was a nasty shock to wake up the next morning to find Nate all dressed and packed and ready to go. He'd decided to leave a day early, he said...."

Her brittle facade shattered. "Oh Mary Jo, I was crazy about him! I even made a fool of myself by telling him so. But he reminded me that we'd agreed 'no strings,' which, of course, I had ignored, just knowing he'd change his mind once we'd been together," she said scathingly. "Then he told me I was wonderful and the weekend was beautiful and thanked me nicely and... walked away."

"And why wasn't he told about the result of his beautiful weekend?" Mary Jo said through gritted teeth.

"Because I couldn't find him. Isn't that funny? After all that talking, I didn't know his address or telephone number or even the name of the company where he worked, just that he lived in Los Angeles. He wasn't listed in the directory. I know because I called every name that even came close—the Nathans, Nats, Nathines, the N. D. Wrights—none of whom were Nate."

Eve finished off her brandy with a tiny shudder. "At that point I didn't even know if he'd given me his right name or the right city. Or maybe he had an unlisted number. Who knows? It didn't matter. Either way, I was on my own. So I said to hell with him—I didn't need Nate Wright and neither did my baby!"

She gave a harsh laugh. "But I was so scared, Mary Jo. Terrified, actually. I had no money, barely eking out an existence. How on earth could I be having a *baby*? We'd taken precautions.... But there it was, a live and growing fact."

Dully she stared at the curtains lifting and falling on the breeze. "So I boarded a bus for home. A long trip by bus, Mary Jo. Lots of time to savor the experience of creeping back home like a whipped puppy, and ample time to imagine the reception I'd get when I arrived. You know how Mother was—"

"Yeah, I know," Mary Jo grunted. "You wouldn't have run off to Vegas in the first place if she hadn't been such a rigid old battle-ax— I'm sorry, Eve, I don't mean to speak ill of the dead," she said contritely. Her small fists clenched. "But Mom told me how she treated you when you came home!"

"Don't, honey. I've made my peace with that. Besides, I wasn't a small-town girl anymore—I much preferred living in Concord." Eve cleared her throat. "I never regretted my decision to keep the baby. For that matter, I can't honestly say I regret meeting Nate, because he gave me my darling Amanda," she ended simply.

"Yes, of course, but . . ." Mary Jo shook her rumpled curls. "I'm still having trouble taking all this in, especially the part about him forgetting you."

"I'm still having a little trouble with that, too," Eve said, painfully wry. "Oh, I know I was a fool, blinding myself to the fact that he was just another man out for a good time in Vegas. But there were times that weekend when I'd swear he held

me as if he wanted something more—as if he could have cared
for me, had he let himself." She shrugged. "A fool, like I said."

"That's another puzzle." Mary Jo sighed, her eyes still dark
and troubled. "I can't picture you as a fool, either. How do you
feel about him now? Do you still love him?"

"No," Eve said flatly.

"Hate him? Resent him?"

"No hatred." Eve stood up and walked to the window. "Not
for years now. I worked hard to build a good life for Amanda
and me, and I wasn't about to let hate and bitterness spoil it.
But resentment . . . yes, some. Oh, Mary Jo, its so unfair! He
walked away untouched, but me . . . You want to know the
loneliest moment of my life? When they laid Amanda in
my arms for the first time and there was no one to share it
with—"

Catching herself up short, Eve jammed her hands into her
pockets. "And then she was so frail and I had such a hard time
of it financially, so I guess a little resentment was natural. But
hate?" She glanced over her shoulder with a tender smile.
"How can I hate what I see every day in Amanda's dear little
face? How can I feel bitter toward him when he gave me the
most precious thing in my life?"

"I guess you can't." Mary Jo mauled her ebony curls as she
studied her cousin's delicate profile. "So now what?"

"I don't know. Nothing, probably." Eve turned. "I've gotten along fine without him thus far. What would I need him for
now?"

"Well, he is loaded, Eve, and you'll be having some heavy
expenses coming up in the future—college for Amanda and all
that," Mary Jo replied pragmatically.

"I can take care of Amanda. Believe me, I know how to
stretch a dollar from here to Concord and back. Besides, if all
I wanted was money, I'd marry my boss. He's crazy about
Amanda and even tolerates me," Eve quipped weakly. "Un-
fortunately he's too nice a man to saddle with a wife who
doesn't absolutely adore him."

"I've often wondered why you didn't snap Brian up," Mary
Jo murmured. She touched Eve's flushed cheek. "Evie, what
you said about being alone when Amanda was born—I'm so

sorry about that. I should have been there for you instead of dashing around all over the place doing my own thing.''

"Your own 'thing' happens to be magnificent and well worth doing," Eve reproved. Mary Jo was an artist. "You said Nate was loaded. How did you know that? Did Patrick talk about him? What did he say?" she asked a shade too eagerly.

"Nothing. I tried to pry but Patrick's a clam," Mary Jo replied disgustedly. "Just deductive reasoning. The watch he wore helped a lot, but mainly it's that air of authority men like him wear like some expensive cologne. And this isn't exactly cheap real estate, Eve. If the owner of this cottage wasn't a friend, we wouldn't be here."

"Hooray for friends," Eve said, yawning. "Well, I'm for bed—I'm beat. Not to mention all wrung out."

"Me, too." Mary Jo began turning off lights. "Is Nate going to call you tomorrow?"

"Yes."

"What are you going to say?"

"I don't know, and I'm too tired to think about it," Eve replied.

Once gowned and in bed, however, the question prowled her mind like a burglar with a master key, unlocking doors and opening sealed chambers until sleep was impossible. Unbidden, her thoughts shot back to Nate and their first time together. She could recall all too well the incandescent haze of sexuality, the time out of time where nothing existed but erotic sensations and hot-blooded feelings. She had been wild for him, on fire with the incredible pleasures he'd taught her.

And he had certainly taught her well, she thought with very bleak humor. Tonight's kiss had proved his talent for programming a woman's body. The passing years had dulled only her memory of the emotions that accompanied their lovemaking.

She had regretted that, for somehow their innocent glory sanctified Amanda's existence. But the sheer intensity of those beautiful feelings made their recapture impossible.

Curling up tighter in her nest of blankets, Eve closed her eyes. She remembered other feelings, too, most not so beautiful. During the weeks after his departure, she had wept her bitter tears, endured the love-hate war that raged in her heart, and went right on hoping, without the slightest reason, that he would return to her.

But these feelings paled to insignificance when she discovered she was carrying his child. She needed him, but she loathed him. Moreover she loathed herself for her inability to stop wanting so desperately a man who didn't want her. Remembering those days, Eve winced. Lord, what an emotional mess she'd been!

But she'd survived, she reminded herself. She'd left Vegas, been thrown out of her mother's house, found herself a job, had her baby and gotten on with her life. What else was there to do?

She'd stopped loving, needing, hating. Ceasing the latter had taken longer, but forcing herself to accept a harsh truth had helped. Nate had neither misled nor deceived her. She'd done that to herself.

Overcoming her bitterness had been another pleasing sign of maturity. All that was left from their brief encounter was her fierce love for the sweet, shy, merry little girl they had created. Her mouth quirked. Why mention the never-ending yearning that haunted her heart? Half the time she didn't know what she was yearning for, anyway.

Another prodigious yawn overtook her. She was so exhausted her bones ached. She curled into a ball and sleepily wondered what she was going to say when Nate called tomorrow.

The wonderful smell of coffee awoke her and led her by the nose downstairs to the kitchen. Eve poured a cup and leaned against the window frame. Her gaze drifted outside to the huge gray boulder, her expression contemplative. The thought of Nate wasn't nearly so disturbing in the sunlight. The day's brightness seemed to dilute the powerful effect he'd had upon her. Either that, or she'd overrated him. Made him bigger than life, she chided herself gently.

More coffee, then Amanda, she decided, refilling her cup. Sipping the hot cream-laced brew, she perched on a stool and reached for the telephone. Her calls home were a joyous though expensive treat.

Amanda was brimming over with news. The cat had had four kittens! Hannah was making sugar cookies! And Amanda had been having a tea party under the apple tree when, for no reason at *all*, a bee 'bit' her.

After pouring on tons of maternal sympathy and outrage at the colossal gall of some bees, Eve ended the rambling conversation with a quick word of reassurance from Hannah, her housekeeper.

Mary Jo strolled in just as Eve hung up the phone, looking like the coming of spring with her armful of flowers. "'Morning. Nate called. He wants you to call him back. The number's on that yellow pad."

"Thanks, honey, but why the somber face?"

"Are you going to see him again?"

"Yes. I've decided I want to try to prod that faulty memory of his," Eve replied lightly. "I repeat, why the somber face?"

"Oh, I don't know." Mary Jo jammed the pink and white chrysanthemums into a vase. "Are you going to tell him about Amanda?"

Eve recoiled. "Good Lord, no! I'm not telling him anything about *anything*." Abashed at her own vehemence, she laughed and tweaked her cousin's snub nose. "Is that what's bothering you?"

"No, not really. I guessed as much. It's just this whole situation confuses me, Eve," Mary Jo burst out. "I liked Nate. He seemed . . . nice, you know? But I guess a lot of guys are like that—nice on the outside and rotten on the inside," she said reflectively, then flung a hand to her mouth. "Oh, Eve, I'm sorry. I forgot I was talking about Amanda's daddy!"

"Don't apologize for the truth, honey. Some guys *are* like that," Eve said, sobering. "Whether Nate's one of them or not is anybody's guess. But since all I want is another shot at improving his memory..." Shrugging, she picked up the receiver. "It's no big deal, Mary Jo."

Despite her airy assurance, Eve's chest grew tighter with each digit dialed. Nate's voice loosened everything again, including her knees.

"Hello, pretty lady!" he said. "I was just about to call you. Patrick and I had planned to do a little fishing this afternoon, and we were just thinking how much more enjoyable it would be if we had something to look at besides the fish we don't catch. So what would you and Mary Jo say to a boat ride?"

"Great! I love boats." Eve said with an inward groan.

"You're out of your mind if you think I'm stepping one foot on a smelly old fishing boat!" Mary Jo said indignantly.

"Oh, don't be a snob, Mary Jo." Eve sniffed. "Could be we might even enjoy it."

Both women were pleasantly surprised at the truth of her words. The "smelly old fishing boat" turned out to be a handsome craft complete with a white-clad crew. Its facilities included a paneled cabin for lunching, a bathroom of sorts—the head, Nat informed her—and a deck for sunbathing, although Nate supposed the brisk sea air would curtail that feminine pleasure.

Eve felt as prickly as a pinecone in Nate's presence. Just act natural, she admonished herself. But it wasn't easy. In his faded jeans and red knit shirt, Nate was arrestingly potently male, and she knew intimately every inch of that handsome physique. Thank goodness for those mirrored dark glasses he wore, she thought. The impersonal air they lent him provided some relief to her tightly coiled nerves.

They strolled to the fishing deck, where, despite her protests, Mary Jo was already seated with a rod in her hands, enduring Patrick's knowing instructions.

"Do you fish?" Nate asked Eve.

"Me? Are you kidding?" She flinched as Patrick dredged up a handful of bait and handed it to Mary Jo. "Yuk!"

"Do you even know now how to fish?" Nate asked exasperatedly. She didn't. He sighed. "I guess I'll have to teach you."

"Don't be ridiculous," she replied haughtily. "I haven't the faintest desire to learn such a messy thing."

"Of course you do," he reproved. "Just climb up in that other chair while I get some bait."

"Nate!" she warned, her voice rising as he reached for a spare bait bucket. "If you think I'm laying one finger on a shrimp that doesn't come with cocktail sauce—"

"Oh, hush and pay attention to the master," he chided.

Eve invited him to take a swim and see if the sharks were hungry. Ignoring the burst of laughter from various listeners, she walked on. Nate followed her. She stopped, turned and bumped into him. He clasped her arms to steady her, then slowly removed his hands.

"Thank you," she said, her breath uneven. The same spicy scent emanating from the sea seemed to cling to the dark hair that had brushed her face. "Aren't you fishing?" she asked.

"I can fish anytime," he replied huskily.

Eve feigned a cough. His words were irrelevant; she knew what that smoky tone of voice was saying. When he sounded like that, she experienced a quick urge to forget everything and just enjoy him. Just surrender to the magic, she thought with a woman's deep longing.

Nate was thinking the same thing, though from a more basic male viewpoint. His blood quickened as she turned in profile. The wind molded her sweatshirt to the proud thrust of her breasts, and white dungarees outlined her round buttocks and sleek thighs. Her slender waist was an exquisite contrast to the ripe flare of hips, her back long and touchingly fragile, centered as it was by that gilded plume of hair. There was a certain lovely swanlike grace to her movements that tugged oddly at his heart.

His breath came faster as she looked up at him. The mouth so near his was slightly parted, moist and enticingly inviting. He knew the taste of it now, knew the delight of that sugary pink tip of tongue circling her upper lip. He had only to bend his head to take it.

He almost did. Only the sudden flash of panic in her eyes stopped him. Panic? Ridiculous, he thought roughly. She had no reason to fear him. The tenderness she evoked in him was damn near tangible.

Her chin snapped up. He laughed—at himself, at her, at the sweetness of what he was feeling. If the defiance in those purple eyes deviated from the ordinary male-female duel of wills, he didn't want to know it.

"Well, come on, woman, let's go find us a beer and a place to talk instead of standing here getting whipped to death by the wind," he blustered.

She donned her sunglasses. "Fine with me. But not inside the cabin. This air is delicious—it's like taking a seltzer bath!"

"I could have done without that image," Nate muttered.

The sheltered spot he found for them permitted a good view of the coastline. For a time their conversation centered around the scenery. Eve said very little and just listened to the pleasing sound of his voice. But Nate soon had enough of that. "Talk to me," he ordered. "I want to know all about you—including what's behind that smile."

Eve's mouth held its ironic curve even though his words had the effect of tiny, sharp-tipped arrows striking her skin. She waited while the steward poured their drinks, a beer for Nate and a diet cola for her, before complying. "I'm the regional manager for a chain of fitness studios. Since I'm also the chain's media spokesperson as well as an aerobics instructor, I keep pretty busy. Too much so, sometimes, but it's a living. A good one, too," she said proudly.

Her pride was justified. That pregnant, flat-broke, terrified girl was now a confident young woman who drove a sporty car, wore nice clothes and owned a small but lovely house complete with a live-in housekeeper.

"Nothing was handed to me, either. I got where I am by hard work and dogged determination," she told him.

"I wouldn't dare suggest otherwise," he said with gentle amusement at the fierceness of her statement.

Flustered, she asked, "How about you? Still making computers?"

Nate's eyebrows winged up. "How did you know I worked with computers?"

Cursing her slip of tongue, Eve cast around for something to cover it. "Oh, well, Patrick, I guess. He must have mentioned it to Mary Jo."

"Umm. Mary Jo must have garbled it then, because that's not what I do," he replied mildly.

Confused, Eve stared at him. The first time she'd asked him what he did, he'd said simply, "I make computers," and dropped the subject. Maybe she ought to drop it, too. "But that's what you used to do," she persisted.

"Yes." He took a drink of beer.

"An electronic-chip wizard," she teased. "Are you going to tell me about it, or is it some deep dark secret?"

"I don't talk about it much...." He smiled. "But no, no deep dark secret. Are you familiar with Starrmark Computers?"

Eve pushed up her glasses. "Who isn't?"

He laughed. "Well, along with a handful of other guys, I helped start that company, in George Starr's garage, in fact. No salaries to speak of, just shares of stock. When we brought out the first model, the market just exploded. We couldn't possibly keep up with the demand! Our decision to work for stock instead of salary became a brilliant move instead of just lack of capital and a lot of faith," he said, warming to the subject as wide violet eyes fixed on his face in rapt attention.

"Nate, that's fantastic!" she said, genuinely impressed. The story of Starrmark Computers was a well-known phenomenon in the business world. That Nate had been part of such an accomplishment added considerably to his persona.

"Yeah, fantastic."

His sardonic tone puzzled Eve. She thought about changing topics, then rejected the notion. "But you don't do that anymore."

"No. About five years ago I left Starrmark and went into software."

Eve diverted her gaze seaward. *About five years ago.*

"That proved to be a pretty smart move, too," he was saying. "Not only do we offer the best software programs on the market, but I don't have to deal with a traffic-jammed commute to and from the office. I run the business from my country estate. Computer room, private office, complete communications system..."

Nate stopped, suddenly hearing himself as she must be hearing him. Good Lord, he was bragging! Trying to impress her like some adolescent, he thought, both amused at himself and surprised that he had let the conversation get so personal.

Ordinarily he was tight-lipped about his private affairs. "Every toy I could possibly want," he ended on a sheepish note.

"Sounds like it," Eve said, smiling. "Where is this grand country estate of yours? California? That is where Starrmark Computers originated, isn't it?"

"Yes, L.A. But I left there when I started my own business. My 'grand estate' is in Portland, Maine."

Is that where you were when I was so desperate to find you? "Why Maine?"

"No particular reason." Stretching, Nate clasped his hands at the back of his head. "It just seemed right."

His tone was dismissive, but Eve pressed on. "Maine's lovely, all that beautiful coastline.... But you bought a place here."

"Does sound odd, doesn't it?" he agreed carelessly. "I've been thinking of selling it. I don't even know why I bought it, to tell the truth. Just one of those urges you get now and then."

An urge that has nothing to do with you, Eve told herself, deriding her heart's flimsy reason for skipping a beat. "Tell me about your Portland home. Do you live there alone?"

"It's a red brick, on a tree-lined avenue. Dusty lives with me. He's sort of my 'man Friday,' though he came with the estate." After a few more desultory comments, Nate stood up. "I think I'd better tell the captain to head back to shore—the sea's getting up a bit," he said, unnecessarily, for Mary Jo was coming toward them with a furious look on her face.

No wonder, Eve thought, suppressing a laugh. A sheet of sea spray had drenched her cousin from head to toe. "Just stuff it, Patrick," Mary Jo snapped at the equally red-faced male who followed her into the cabin. Patrick wasn't all that dry himself, but apparently that didn't count. Snatching up her beach bag, Mary Jo stomped off to a bedroom to change clothes while he flopped down in a canvas chair in the living room.

Eve made a commiserating face, but decided against joining him. When Nate returned from the bridge, she was standing by the rail combing her loosened hair with her fingers.

"You look so pretty with your hair blowing in the wind like that," he said, threading a finger through the golden mass.

She looked up at him and his chest tightened. He hated the wariness he saw in her beautiful eyes. It would give him great pleasure to meet the man who'd put it there!

"Eve, have dinner with me tonight."

Eve gave herself thirty seconds to deliberate. "Sure, why not? We have to eat somewhere," she said, knowing she was baiting a very healthy male ego but unable to resist. "Where shall we meet you?"

His brow arched. " 'We'?"

"Of course. Aren't Mary Jo and Patrick included?"

Nate's fine mouth formed a sardonic twist. "Looks that way. Pick you up around seven?"

"Oh, we'll get ourselves there. Just tell me where."

"What's with this 'get ourselves there' bit?" he asked irritably. "You even 'got yourselves' down to the dock today."

Her voice cooled. "I'm sorry if that annoys you, but I happen to like having my own car. That way I can always leave when I want to. We could compromise, though," she added as he stepped away from her.

He reached for the cabin door. "We could also forget it."

"No." Eve caught his arm, a reflex reaction that startled her into a quick laugh. "I don't want to forget it."

He stared at her. Then, slowly, his hard jaw relaxed.

"Neither do I. So what's your compromise?"

"I'll pick *you* up. We will, I mean. Seven o'clock?"

Two curving lines carved his cheeks. "Sure, why not? We have to eat somewhere."

His dry humor tickled Eve into another spontaneous laugh.

Enjoying it, Nate linked his fingers with hers. "Tell me, Ms. Sheridan, what's your favorite dinner?"

"Endive salad, crunchy rolls, broiled lobster and French fries," Eve replied promptly.

"And your favorite flower?"

Her fingers left his. "Forget-me-nots."

"Um. Second favorite?"

"I like all flowers," she said with a shrug.

About then Mary Jo reappeared, scrubbed and combed and crisply cute in nautical whites. Patrick, of course, still wore his grubby fishing outfit. Her nose tilted three inches higher than usual as he rose to stand beside her.

"Nate," she called, "are we nearly home? I've had about all of this kind of fun I can take. Patrick, would you mind standing downwind a bit? A mile or so should do it."

Patrick's response, though clearly plaintive, was inaudible to Eve. All she heard was Nate's rich chuckle. It poked around inside her until it unearthed a memory of another such chuckle rumbling against her bare skin. *"I don't believe I've ever seen a birthmark quite like this before...."*

"You've gotten awfully quiet," Mary Jo remarked as she and Eve drove back to the cottage.

Sighing, Eve rubbed her neck. "Just tired."

Mary Jo glanced at her. "Eve, I know you feel this afternoon didn't accomplish much—"

"Don't sugarcoat, Mary Jo. This afternoon accomplished nothing."

"Oh, I wouldn't say that," Mary Jo protested.

"I would. But then, you know how cranky I get when I'm tired," Eve drawled, regretting her sharpness.

"I know. Being with Nate must be a big strain on you.... That's why I was so surprised about us going out with them tonight, especially since he didn't show any signs of remembering you. But I guessed you wanted to give it one more try."

Eve smiled. Close enough, she thought.

"I'm glad we're taking our car, though," her cousin went on. "Saves us the hassle of a good-night kiss."

"My sentiments exactly," Eve said, forcing a laugh.

Irritably she wondered why she had to force anything, which led to the admission of Nate's effect on her nerves.

But a luxurious soak in a steamy bath, followed by a vigorous rubdown, rejuvenated both body and spirit. "Hope springs eternal," she muttered to the mirror. "No matter how hopeless."

Sun and wind had given her normally fair complexion a rosy glow. Deciding to accentuate its radiance, she selected a hot-pink silk shell and navy harem pants. A silver lamé belt cinched her trim waist. The curved matching jacket, lined in the same vibrant pink silk, was perfect for the cool night air.

Ten minutes of self-admonition and encouragement completed her ensemble. By seven she felt ready to return to the arena.

Nate's house was a beautiful composition of glass, fieldstone and redwood, with a commanding view of the sea. Eve would have liked to have seen the inside of it, but he and Patrick were waiting on the terrace.

"This is gorgeous, Nate!" Mary Jo exclaimed.

Eve agreed, but she didn't trust her voice enough to say so. Her first sight of Nate had created a hole where her stomach ought to be. The sunglasses were gone, and his intense gray gaze was flickering over and around her like heat lightning working its way inland.

The flash of corresponding warmth seemed to sizzle through her veins. Simultaneously, she felt a chill ripple under her skin. She hadn't overrated him. For an overwhelming instant that spun out forever, all in the world she wanted to do was to run to him and beg him to hold her.

Three

___

Patrick's bantering voice jerked Eve back to reality. He was telling Mary Jo that she resembled a wood's elf in that green thingamajig she had on. Eve took a deep breath and made herself laugh. Relax, she ordered. Or pretend, if you have to. Just don't let Nate see what he does to you. And don't underestimate him anymore.

The *him* she referred to had uncoiled from his chair and was sauntering toward her, a light gray sport jacket slung over one shoulder. Charcoal-gray slacks and a sky-blue turtleneck sweater stressed the clean lines of his body. His hair was still damp from his shower, and he smelled, she decided, like a breath of forest air.

Poised to the teeth, nerves taut and alert, she tilted her head. "Hi, Nate," she said.

His gray eyes crinkled. "Hello, Eve."

Her heart jumped. How could he put so much into a simple greeting? "Have you decided yet where we're eating tonight?" she asked testily. "It might help to know since I'm driving."

"Cables," he replied, eyes twinkling.

"Cables? Well!" Mary Jo said, looking impressed. "Let's go, then. I'm starved!"

"What's Cables?" Eve asked as they started back to the car.

"Pure class and fabulous food," Mary Jo answered. "Or so I've heard, since I haven't actually been there. Do I have to sit in back with Patrick?" she appealed to Eve.

"Oh hush and get in," Patrick growled. "Why is Eve driving?" he asked Nate.

"Because I want her to, of course," Nate answered.

Eve gave him a considering look, but decided to let it pass.

Cables was located in an old reconverted mansion. Its entrance was lined with flowers, wicker love seats and people waiting for tables. Nate's party, however, was immediately ushered to one of the semiprivate dining rooms.

After being seated, Eve shared a raised-eyebrows glance with Mary Jo, then looked around with a silent purr of pleasure. The candlelit room was a visual melody of shimmering crystal and silver, dusky rose walls and ice-pink napery. Champagne nestled in a silver cooler. The two pristine white roses lying across their plates necessitated another shared look.

A smile played over Nate's mouth as he watched Eve. Her wandering gaze met his and held as she languidly raised the rose to her lips. Leaning toward her, he inhaled the perfumed warmth that surrounded her like an elusive mist and murmured, "I couldn't find forget-me-nots. I hope you like champagne with your favorite meal?"

Violet eyes sparkling above the rose's pure white petals suddenly resembled ice-glazed amethysts. Then, with chameleon quickness, the chill vanished in a throaty little laugh. "I've liked good champagne since I was nineteen."

Eve was already regretting giving in to her swift anger, however briefly. She didn't let her emotions rule her; she ruled them. To her relief, the puzzled look on Nate's face disappeared as she added, "These roses are lovely."

"Everything's lovely," Mary Jo said. "But I am curious to know when you made these reservations, Patrick."

"This morning."

Eve's mouth opened, then closed as the wine steward seemingly materialized out of the woodwork. While he poured the champagne, a waitress brought warm fragrant rolls and a tiny china plate set in a woven silver basket.

"Pâté de foie gras," Patrick told Mary Jo grandly. "The roses and champagne were Nate's idea, but this is mine. I ordered it just for you."

"Big deal," she snorted, practically inhaling the luscious stuff. "Strip away that fancy name and what have you got? Fattened goose livers. And just how did you know this morning that we'd be here with you this evening?"

"Good question," Eve said, glancing at Nate. "Do you have an answer that won't leave you sitting here with just Patrick and fattened goose livers?"

"Hope," said Nate promptly. "Hope and pulling petals off a daisy. It came out 'she will.' An omen I couldn't ignore."

"No sane man could," Patrick agreed.

Laughter circled their table like scarlet ribbons. From that point on, Eve found her prickly self tangled up in a web of enjoyment that ran the gamut from the ridiculous to the sublime. The champagne was buoyancy in a bottle, the French cuisine rich and delectable, her companions entertaining. Mary Jo and Patrick were soon embroiled in another argument, and each sought backup from time to time. Nate was a formidable ally. His sexy gray eyes gleamed with mischief as he threw in just enough provocative comments to drag Eve into their absurdity.

The mutual esteem and affection that flowed between the two men was heartwarming. They might have known each other all their lives, Eve thought aloud.

"We met nine or ten years ago—in a bar, if I remember right," Nate said. "Patrick took exception to some sumo wrestler's remark, and I had to come to the rescue." He lifted his glass in a toast. "Here's to old friends and new, and especially to those just met."

The gesture of touching glasses was curiously solemn for all its festive air. Incredible, Eve thought, that four strangers had formed such an easy bond in such a short time.

Considering that she had borne his child, it seemed absurd to think of Nate as a stranger. But it didn't feel absurd. The man she remembered had been, for the most part, quiet and

sober natured, his manner subtly aloof. Even on the boat today his humor had seemed strained and awkward. Confronting this laughing, teasing, marvelously relaxed male was as
unsettling as anything she'd ever experienced.

Furthermore, he was courting her, she realized with a sham-
ing thrill. She had thought herself too mature for such sopho-
moric romanticism. Instead she found it a heady stimulant that
satisfied a need she hadn't known existed until now.

Inwardly she grimaced. The very idea of an unknown need
was disconcerting. She knew her needs—after all that soul-
searching, she knew herself inside and out! Too much champagne, that was it. They'd finished off two bottles during their
leisurely meal. Although, after one glass, Nate had stuck to
sparkling water.

Realizing he was speaking to her, Eve looked at him blankly.
"After-dinner drinks," Mary Jo supplied. Eve chose an Irish
coffee. Nate requested their order be brought to the bar.

The appropriately dim room featured live entertainment.
Eyeing the frenzied fertility rites taking place on the dance
floor, Eve wished she'd left the Irish out of her coffee. The
music was hot and smoky. So were Nate's eyes. And so was the
wild, sweet defiance singing through her blood.

She knew the danger; each beat of her heart shredded a little more of the reserve that was such a vital part of her defenses. It made her uneasy, but there wasn't much she could do
about it except remind herself that it was only for one night.
Nate was already whirling her off to the dance floor.

He had discarded his jacket and pushed up his sleeves. The
big vibrant male threw back his head and laughed, eyes gleaming, as Eve danced circles around him. She felt safe; they didn't
touch. But when a soft lilting ballad managed to infiltrate the
band's instruments, her sense of security vanished the instant
Nate drew her into his embrace.

She felt captured. The world around her was falling away, its
sounds becoming muted. Her lashes came swiftly down, a
protective screen that shielded her reaction to the hands sliding slowly down her back. The long fingers moved to press her
closer in clever ways that gave her the delicious details of his
lean frame. She shivered as something tickled her spine. Hot-

and-cold running thrills, she realized distractedly. His heat seemed to permeate her body and fuse it to the steel of muscle and bone and warm, hard flesh.

Suddenly devoid of grace, she stepped on his foot. "I'm sorry," she said, and did it again. "Damn!"

"It's all right, Eve." Nate bent his head and trailed his mouth along the curve of her cheek to her ear. "Just relax and let the music take you," he whispered.

Dangerously tempted, Eve shifted her viewpoint to clinical observation, a trick she had taught herself when feeling overwhelmed. Deliberately she recalled the first time he'd held her like this. The sensations she was experiencing were very similar. But the similarity was reassuring rather than alarming. Perhaps because there were no emotional overtones, no burgeoning, rapturous certainty that she'd found true love. *This* was strictly physical, she concluded sardonically.

Then, as now, Nate possessed the sensuous excitement of dark good looks, strong adept hands and a masculine power made all the more potent by its balancing tenderness.

And now, as then, Eve knew it would feel so good to just close her eyes and savor the erotic friction generated by their swaying movements. Instead she tensed and inadvertently sent a spiky heel raking across his instep.

When the dance ended, she refused another. "I don't know why you'd even want to try again, the way I stepped all over your feet," she said somewhat crossly.

"I can't believe you stepped on his feet," a slightly tipsy Mary Jo chimed in. "I mean, she was a dancer," she told Patrick. "A professional dancer," she stressed when he failed to look suitably impressed. "In Vegas."

Patrick's eyes rounded gratifyingly. "Were you really?"

"You were a chorus-line dancer?" Nate asked, unsurprised at his lack of surprise. That lovely grace of hers, those long good legs and supple body all added up.

"Yes, Patrick, I was a chorus-line dancer," she mimicked. Her gaze glanced off Nate's. " 'Was' being the operative word here. That's ancient history," she said negligently, but Nate saw a hint of the Arctic in her smile and a subtle sharpness in her features, as if the skin had drawn tighter around them.

She's a riddle within a riddle, Nate thought. But he dropped it. For now.

At Eve's request, they left shortly afterward. "I'm driving," Nate stated, steering her toward the passenger seat. Though his arbitrary decision evoked a frown, she didn't challenge it. "I'll drop you two off rather than the other way around," he continued as they started driving down the street. "We'll get the car to you in the morning."

She laid her head back against the seat. "As you wish. I have a feeling that's the way it's going to be, anyway."

The puckish humor in her voice wrung a deep chuckle from Nate. But she sat far removed from him, and he couldn't stand that, not when his entire body stung with wanting to touch her. Capturing her hand, he rested it on his thigh and wove their fingers together, tugging gently, until he had moved her close enough to ignite his senses with her fragrance.

"I wanted you to have a wonderful time tonight," he said, very low. "I really tried to see that you did."

"I did have a wonderful time, Nate. And I wasn't blind to your efforts, believe me. In fact, I was impressed."

"Even though you didn't want to be," he said, but his voice had a humorous little flicker in it.

"Even though," she agreed.

After that they drove in silence, each absorbed in private thoughts, and each grateful, Eve suspected, for the mild backseat bickering that filled the gap. The glow of the dashboard light imparted a moody sensuality to Nate's profile. She wondered what he was thinking and what he would say if he could read her mind. *"You were a chorus-line dancer?"*

Two in the morning.

Eve tossed aside the book of poetry she was reading and rubbed her gritty eyes. The bedroom she had chosen was serenely decorated in the softest pinks and creams. But nothing, not Keats nor a goose-down comforter, could soothe her agitated spirit. Her fingers still tingled from Nate's possessive clasp, and there was a tormenting deep-seated ache inside her. With a resigned sigh, she left the rumpled bed and stepped out onto the balcony.

A witch's caldron of scent and sight and sound assaulted her senses. The sky was black and starless. A rumbling barrage of long, white-toothed combers crashed upon the shore. The night wind tasted of rain and dark foreign places. It whipped her hair and lifted her gown like some ghostly male presence. It reached low inside her to expose longings she didn't want and a sadness she couldn't explain.

At least the ache was identifiable, Eve thought, dry humored. Her body remembered his, solid and excitingly defined beneath his clothing. Her mind remembered him without clothes, each hard plane and sinew of him, stroking, caressing, melting bone and flesh alike.

When she had lain in Nate's arms, every fiber of her body had known that she was a woman. She wanted to know it again. But she wanted something else more—to love with all her passionate heart and be loved in return.

Such a simple desire, so natural. So unobtainable. She had yet to meet a man who could inflame her emotions the way Nate had. Not even her employer, Brian Oliver, whom she liked and trusted more than any other man, could do that.

Sometimes she wondered at herself. Brian was forty, a gruff, sweet, teddy bear of a man, who, although treasuring their friendship as much as she, would nevertheless like to make her his wife. Accepting him as her life's companion wouldn't be all that difficult, especially since he got on well with Amanda—a top priority to Eve. He was the only man she permitted her child to call uncle.

But Nate was Amanda's father, she thought. He should be the one—

No! Eve froze and gripped the rail, feeling with panic her swift, joyous response to that uncompleted thought. Something had shattered inside her. She felt it happen, felt a defensive wall she'd worked years to build crumble in a moment's time. The foolish dream she'd thought dead and buried had suddenly come alive.

It had stolen into her unguarded mind the night her daughter was born, an indelible wish-image her heart still harbored in defiance of hard-learned realism. *Eve and Nate and their child, together, a family.*

The ultimate happily ever after. Eve jeered at her fantasy, blinking furiously. As if to match her inner storm, white lightning zigzagged across the black sky. Seconds later, a whip-crack of thunder violated the night. She fled back to the sanctuary of her bed.

Rain pelted the windowpanes. Snapping out the light, Eve rolled into a blanketed cocoon and continued her self-argument. It hurt to deride such lovely illusions, but she couldn't afford to fantasize, not about Nate. Stirring up the moldy dust of old wants and needs was both stupid and dangerous.

But what if, a persistent inner voice whispered, *what if there was a chance—a slight chance, true, but still a chance—that the foolish little dream that would not die turned out to be not so foolish, after all?*

Eve awoke to a world of washed blue skies and sunshine. She wasn't surprised to see it was nearly ten o'clock; dawn had grayed her windows before she'd slept. What did surprise her was how strong she felt. The vigorous thirty-minute workout she performed each morning scarcely made a dent in her energy.

She stripped off her leotard, intending to shower, but the smell of coffee was becoming irresistible. "Caffeine fiend," she muttered. Throwing on a long pink wrapper, she nearly flew down the stairs. "Mary Jo? You about the house?" she called as she filled a thick white mug.

"No, but I am," a resonant male voice replied from the vicinity of the deck.

Whirling, Eve gasped as a tall figure dressed in black sweatpants and shirt appeared at the kitchen's screened door. "Good morning," Nate said.

"Oh! Ouch! Good morning! Blast!" Eve sputtered, shaking her coffee-splashed fingers. "Nate, come in. What are you doing here? Where's Mary Jo? Coffee?" Oh God, my hair, she thought, pushing at the disheveled gold mass spilling around her shiny face. Bare toes . . . I'm barefoot! And there's nothing under this robe. After that workout, I probably smell awful. Do I smell awful? "I just woke up," she said lamely.

"So I see," he said, stepping inside. Impossibly, his voice deepened. "You're beautiful when you just wake up, Eve Sheridan."

A memory tore loose, sharp and vivid. Same words, another time and place. Her hands trembled. Setting down the cup, she wiped her fingers with a kitchen towel and carefully rehung it on a rack.

"Thank you. You didn't answer my questions. How long have you been out there?"

"Coffee, please. Black with sugar. I've been here about five minutes. Patrick drove Mary Jo to the store. I decided to take a run down the beach, then wait here for you." His voice softened to sensual velvet. "As for why I'm here, maybe I just wanted to see you like this."

Without seeming to move, he was suddenly so near that his breath caressed her upturned face. Eve could taste his intent even before he bent his head. Her back was against the counter. With a quick step sideways, she eased around him and out of temptation's path. "I'll get your coffee, then I'm going upstairs and get dressed," she said matter-of-factly.

"Not on my account, I hope." He sat down at the table, his gaze bright and hot upon her. "Come, sit down. At least have a cup of coffee with me before you run off," he said with a lazy male arrogance that was guaranteed to ignite her pride.

"I wasn't *running* anywhere, Nate." Tossing her head, she tightened her sash and sauntered to the coffeepot.

Nate watched her, chin propped in hand, his mouth distracting her with its tenderness. His gaze fell to the toes peeping from the hem of her robe. "I can't picture you as a chorus girl," he said musingly. "There's something about you that just won't mesh with the image those words conjure up."

Eve's mind faltered for only a heartbeat. "A stereotype image, of course—brazen hussies without morals, hopping in and out of beds like hungry fleas!"

Her amused drawl had an edge. The arch of his dark brows flattened slightly. "Stereotypes do exist. Especially in the places that make them."

"Oh, come on. I met some very nice ladies there." She handed him a mug of coffee, then took the opposite chair. "We weren't all party dolls to be played with and then discarded like some boring toy." Catching herself up short, she managed a convincing chuckle. "But men don't go there to meet ladies, do they? Take yourself. How often do you wing off to Vegas for a fun-filled weekend?"

"I've been there," he conceded. "But not all men go there to collect fleas. Sometimes they just need to relax, take a break from their troubles, their work, their women, whatever. Speaking for myself, I happen to enjoy gambling."

"Did you go back?" Eve paused, trying to think of some innocuous way to ask her gnawing question. *Did you go back after I left?* "I mean recently."

"No, it's been a while. Several years, in fact. When were you there?" he asked, obviously intrigued by this provocative chapter of her life.

"Five or six years ago. I've lost count." Looking down, she stirred her coffee. Lying always made her feel queasy and certain she looked that way. She cleared her throat. "I wasn't there all that long. Less than a year, in fact, before I . . . faced reality and called it quits. Not because I lacked talent—I was quite good, actually. Not good enough, though." Honesty compelled her to continue. "I doubt I'd ever have gotten a chance if the owner of the club hadn't been a family acquaintance."

Wrapping both hands around her cup, she inhaled the coffee's rich aroma. Why was she telling him all this? Because he was hanging on to her every word. Vanity, thy name is danger, she quipped defiantly.

"I did have talent, but I also had problems. I couldn't adjust, I couldn't conform. Everything I'd been taught to believe in seemed so . . . corny, I guess. And those skimpy costumes . . ." She grimaced. "Every time I pranced out on the stage, all I could think of was what my mother would say. What she *did* say."

"Not too happy with your chosen career, hmm?"

"She was appalled. And ashamed," Eve said, gazing out to sea. "Women have such dreams for their daughters. Nice dreams, tremendous dreams. But mine wasn't hers. And hers wasn't mine. I thought her ideas were too simplistic and old-fashioned. I was too immature to realize that the old-fashioned only endures because it's been proven worthy." Her gaze refocused on his quiet face. "Oh well, I was young and full of myself. At least I had the sense to put away my fond illusions and 'get real,' as Mary Jo puts it."

"I wouldn't say you're too old for fond illusions even now. You're still just a girl," he teased. "What—nineteen, twenty?"

Eve smiled briefly, knowing that he was joking. "Twenty-five soon. And I stopped being a girl long before I ever reached twenty."

"What happened when you were twenty?"

"I grew up in a hurry," she said dismissively. "You ever been married?" she asked, knowing he had, but it was a question women would normally ask.

He sipped his coffee. "Once."

"What happened?" That, she didn't know.

"Things went sour." A shadow chased across his face. "It ended badly."

"And now I suppose you're burned-out on marriage."

"Maybe a little, I don't know. But I prefer to think I just haven't found anyone else I cared for to that extent." An eyebrow danced up. "What's your excuse?"

"I don't need an excuse. Sometimes women find it easier to go it alone, that's all. But I do enjoy a good friendship, like the one I have now, at home."

Nate's eyes narrowed. "Obviously you're not in love with him, or you wouldn't be here with me."

"I'm not here with you. You're here with me," she pointed out. "But you're right. Head over heels in love is another illusion I discarded years ago. And it's not an exclusive relationship because I don't want to get that serious. Yet." She stood up. "By the way, Mary Jo has her own dream. You might mention that to Patrick, because it does not include getting romantically involved." An odd smile tucked into her mouth. "Sometimes dreams are dangerous things. Especially when they get the upper hand. If you'll excuse me, I'm going to shower and dress." Turning, she walked swiftly toward the staircase. "Help yourself to more coffee, if you like," she called over her shoulder.

Eve held on to the rail as she mounted the stairs. Her legs weren't as stable as when she'd come down. When she reached the top, she stopped and listened. The screen door banged shut. Her breath leaked out in a long sigh.

She was sitting on the window seat drying her hair when Mary Jo slumped in. "Straighten up, Mary Jo," she chided automatically. "You got a spare minute? I need to talk to you."

"I need to talk to you, too." Mary Jo sighed, dropping into a velvet wing chair. "But you first."

"It's about Nate," Eve plunged right in. "I did a lot more thinking than sleeping last night, and came to some decisions. One is to overlook his lapse of memory."

"How on earth can you do that?" Mary Jo asked, incredulous.

Eve hesitated, knowing she still had to deal with the stinging fact and accept the obvious: she had been easy to leave and easy to forget. The iron that time and circumstance had stitched into her backbone stiffened. "Because I have to. It's a fact, and one has to accept facts."

"Or change them."

"You mean tell him? I'd die first." Wrapped in a tangerine bath sheet, Eve rose and began pacing. "I didn't say I'd forget it—I doubt it will ever be far from mind. But I can handle it. I have to, because I'm going to continue seeing Nate. Wait, let me finish," she said, forestalling her cousin's question. "Look, Amanda needs a father, don't you agree? Nate is her father, but he doesn't know it. And won't, not until I discern his true character. And approve of it, of course. Even then he'd have to pass a lot of tests—"

"And what about you? What if you get hurt again?"

"I won't. And in any case, I'm not a piece of fragile china, Mary Jo, so stop with the worried looks, okay? Remember what Mother always said—"

"'Pain builds character!'" they chorused in unison.

Chuckling, Eve went on. "But it's not as if this is a do-or-die thing—I can break it off anytime I choose. All I really want is to find out if he's worthy of knowing his child. Simple."

"And if he is?"

"If he is, well, one step at a time. That's how I coped with everything else."

"But how are you going to act with him?" Mary Jo asked curiously.

"As if we've just met," Eve said after a thoughtful pause. "In a sense, we have. I don't really know him. But I do need help, honey. I've got to form some intelligent impressions, and right now I can't be objective about anything when I'm alone with him. I need time to find my footing, so stick with me for a few more days?" she appealed.

"Yes, of course...." Mary Jo stared at her, a pleased smile of realization dawning on her face. "Eve, you're leaning on me, aren't you!"

"Why, yes, I guess I am," Eve said with a startled laugh. "Do you mind?"

Dark eyes shone. "I guess I can bear it, being as how we're friends as well as cousins," Mary Jo replied consideringly. "But just remember, Eve, there *is* a limit to friendship."

For the next few days, the jolly threesome—and sometimes foursome, if Patrick drove down from Portland—explored the town's nightlife as well as its daytime attractions.

Like a benediction, the beautiful weather held. This particularly warm, sunny afternoon had encouraged a picnic. Mary Jo sat sketching under a wind-twisted oak; Eve and Nate lounged nearby, engaged in conversation. Nothing controversial, just things Nate had heard before but didn't remember, Eve thought with the thin, ironic smile that perplexed him so. Increasing familiarity didn't lessen the guarded distance she kept between them. Nate accepted it, for she was a lovely challenging mystery to him.

He watched her constantly, not knowing exactly what he was watching *for* until she tilted her lips to unveil a wry little dimple or quirked an eyebrow quizzically, which enthralled him all the more. The legend of Circe isn't so farfetched after all, he thought, amused at his predictable reaction.

At length she wandered off to speak with Mary Jo, then collected a diet drink from the small ice chest, seemingly indifferent to the hooded gray eyes observing her every movement.

Idly, intensely, Nate studied the cascade of shining hair streaming down her back. There was such a quaint primness about her. Like a good little girl trying earnestly to be what she thought she ought to be, he reflected fondly. And beneath that primness, trapped like a flower under a sheet of ice, glowed the sensuality he ached to set free.

Other things about her made him ache. Her untouchable aura, for one. With the brief exception of their evening at Cables, her demeanor was cool and courteous. But every now and then, when that guarded reserve shattered and a spontaneous gaiety broke through, he'd catch a glimpse of another Eve, a bewitchingly sexy, mischievous, uninhibited temptress he wanted devoutly to know better.

Why she seemed so bent on concealing this captivating side of her personality was just another puzzle. She glanced up at him just then, and her quick smile wrapped around his heart like spun-gold cobwebs. It was an extraordinary sensation. But then, she was an extraordinary woman. She looked fragile, yet he sensed in her a solid core of strength, like finely tempered steel. It didn't take much to guess that someone had hurt her—and he wouldn't mind at all getting his hands on that someone's neck.

He saw the lacy fringe of lashes conceal her eyes as she sat down beside him. Unable to contain his wonder any longer, he asked abruptly, "Who was he? The man who destroyed your illusions. Did you love him?"

She stilled. Then, visibly relaxing, she replied lightly, "I thought so. In fact, I thought I'd die when he walked out. But I seem to have survived without too much damage."

"Who was he?" Nate repeated, his voice and glinting eyes a textural match.

"His name was Bax. My high school sweetheart, believe it or not. It was after I came home from Vegas," Eve said, impulsively deciding to blend two separate events. At that time she had been desperately seeking an emotional base, and Bax had seemed the answer. "It was wonderful at first. But being on my own had changed me quite a bit, while he, well, he'd gone from football star to driving an eighteen-wheeler without ever growing up." She shifted uncomfortably. "This can't be exciting for you. Let's change subjects."

Nate's caressing touch on her cheek startled her with its warmth. "All right. What would you say to cutting out and finding a dark little place that serves fantastic food along with romantic music?"

"I thought we'd go back to Cables—it was lots of fun," Eve evaded the question. "Didn't you enjoy it?"

Baffled annoyance sheened his eyes before she heard his easy laugh. "Yes, I did. But Eve, there seems to be something missing from our relationship. Like romance and candlelight dinners for two, just the tiniest hint of unbridled passion..." Exasperated humor laced his voice. "And at this rate, it threatens to become too well established for my liking!"

Together they watched his big hand cover hers, his fingers so strong and tanned against the pale softness of hers. "I want to be alone with you, Eve. I want, very much, to do the normal, natural things two people do when they're attracted to each other." He withdrew his hand. "Unless, of course, one of them doesn't feel the same way?"

Eve's throat tightened. "You know better than that."

"I thought I did," he agreed evenly. "But so far you've kept a very noticeable distance between us. Sometimes when you walk away from me and then look back over your shoulder with just enough promise to tempt me onward, I feel like I'm on some kind of a leash. It's not a feeling I'm accustomed to, but it's incredibly exciting."

His shoulders went back. The dark head lifted with unmistakable authority. "Up to a point. We've passed that point, Eve. It's time we got to know each other."

Four

Her lashes swept down in that familiar way. Nate's heart softened. He knew it signified a quiet withdrawal to give her time to think. He had first noticed this endearing trait during their evening at Cables, and it never failed to stir him.

Then Eve looked up and laughed, her eyes sparkling, though with what, he didn't know. "That's what we've been doing, Nate—getting to know each other. Without bedroom gymnastics to clutter up our perceptions." She brushed a fingertip across his lips, causing a most incredible sensation at the back of his mouth. "I never do anything without a purpose, and that, Mr. Wright, was it."

"I see. Did I pass whatever test you were giving me?"

"You did, but it was a very limited test."

"In that case, what would you say to a romantic candlelight dinner, some soft music and a healthy dollop of unbridled passion?"

Under her sun-kissed skin, a deeper color blossomed. "About that unbridled passion bit—"

"Oh, hell." He sighed, looking disappointed. "No unbridled passion, then. I'll go with plan two. Dinner out, then some very fine wine and a fire to go with it—in my den, of course—sparkling conversation, a stolen kiss or two—" he grinned "—bridled, of course."

How wonderful it would be had they just met, Eve thought with poignant sorrow. But they hadn't, and all her wishful yearning could not turn back the clock—a chilling fact she tried to keep uppermost in her mind like a string tied around her finger.

He raised her hand to his lips. "Shall we?"

"I can't think of a single reason why we shouldn't," she heard herself saying.

Eve thought of several reasons they shouldn't have later that evening. Dinner went well, but returning to his place had put a strain on her vow to act as if they'd just met and this was their first date. Nervously she toyed with her hair, disliking the silence, yet loath to break it.

"What are you thinking?" Nate asked quietly.

"Oh, all sorts of things," she replied with a bright smile. Curling deeper into her chair, she stared into the hauntingly lovely traces of color that flickered through the driftwood fire. Nate sat across from her, rolling an empty brandy snifter between his big hands. A snowy linen shirt and tailored black trousers hugged the contours of his tall body. With his tousled dark hair and the unruly sideburns framing his strong cheekbones, he was the picture of raw masculinity. Every nerve in her body was screaming its feminine response.

Uneasily she gazed around the cheerful room. Though his home was more luxurious than the cottage, it was also more homey. More suited to a child. The thought startled Eve. She glanced at Nate, then hastily returned her attention to the multicolored flames.

Nate stretched his long legs, his hooded gaze smoldering with a different fire. Unable to bear the warmth of it, Eve got up and walked to the huge window that overlooked a moonlit ocean.

"It's so lovely," she whispered. "And so seductively dangerous."

Murmuring agreement, Nate watched her broodingly, his gaze dark with yearning. Her slightest move was glossed with sensuality. He could taste her mouth like a memory on his tongue. A low-cut black dress graced her slim curvacious figure. Her hair coiled in a Grecian knot high at the back of her head, leaving an off-center cascade to lie against her skin like silken harvest sheaves.

Eve: eternal woman. Soft, secretive, bewitching. Nate was standing behind her before he was aware of moving from his chair.

He heard her soft catch of breath as he kissed her shoulder. Tenderness swamped him. With exaggerated care, he gathered her hair to one side and let his lips swirl across her nape. Her skin was warm, sweet tasting, exotically fragrant. Desire spiraled through him. The curves caressing the front of his body stiffened as an arm around her middle pulled her hard against him, but his need was strong, so strong.

"Don't, please," she said sharply.

"Why not, Eve?" came his low question.

"Because you're turning my knees to water, and I don't much like that. Oh Nate..." She sighed as his breath brushed her skin like a velvet whisk.

She was afraid, and yet she was not. The sweetness of familiarity blunted her wariness. She knew so many intimate things about him: the way his voice thickened to a rasp of passion at the moment of peak excitement, where he liked to be touched, his need to hold and be held afterward....

But she still knew very little about the man himself. Although he seemed decent, everyone wore a disguise, Eve reminded herself cynically. She had lost her head once, let her heart and body overrule a reasonably intelligent brain. She told herself firmly that she was not about to be caught in that same honeyed trap.

And even while she did so, she was turning to face him, her lips already parting in anticipation of his kiss.

His head lowered. Powerful arms drew her tightly against his body. He kissed the curve of one cheek, then trailed his lips from her temple to her throat and the frantic pulse throbbing in its tender hollow. Feather light, his mouth traveled up and over her chin and then along the other cheek.

His every touch is magic, she thought through the befuddling haze of it.

Resentment pierced her. Delight wiped it away. Eve shuddered once and lifted her mouth to his in eager invitation.

"Ah honey, how I've wanted this," she heard him whisper. Then with impassioned demand, his mouth came to hers and made it his.

The scorching hunger in his kiss consumed thought and reason. Eve wasn't prepared for the tumultuous rush of feeling or for the quick, bright urgency flaring throughout her body. Stretching on tiptoes, she pressed against the taut muscularity of his thighs, mindlessly seeking to cool the aching heat of her desire.

The telephone's harsh peal was a jarring intrusion. It rang again and again before Nate lifted his head with a muttered oath. She felt him shudder as he caught her bruisingly tight for a moment. Then, reluctantly, he set her from him.

Eve's laugh was a wonder to her ears. "Saved by the bell!" she said breathlessly.

"Yeah. I'd like to strangle that bell," Nate growled.

Grateful for its support, Eve sank down on the couch. As soon as she realized that the call was business rather than social, she lost interest in it. The heady swirl of feelings still quivering in her stomach had first priority. She was trying to sort them out when an abrupt change in Nate's voice snapped her to alertness.

"When?" he asked tersely. Listening, he shook his head, the muscles in his jaw tight and squared. He was facing her, and Eve sat up with a silent gasp. His eyes were cold, gray granite.

It was the first time she had seen him angry, and the steely force of it raised the fine hairs on the back of her neck as his voice lowered to flat command. "No. No compromises, no concessions. He should have thought of his family before.... That's his problem, Patrick, not ours." He glanced at Eve. "We'll finish this discussion when I get in," he said, and hung up.

Eve steadied her voice. "You're leaving?"

"Yes, tonight, in fact."

"Something's wrong, I take it."

He flicked her a glance. "Yes, something's wrong. Nothing that can't be handled, though."

"Obviously you intend doing just that, and none too kindly," she ventured.

Nate's laugh chilled her. "Not too kindly, no."

"I don't know what he's done, but you said something about his having a family—"

"Yes, he's got a family, and I've got a code of ethics, ethics that I respect in others and that *I* expect to be respected in turn." He plowed a hand through his hair. "Look, I apologize for this. But Patrick has been trying to call me all evening, and this really is important." A thin smile broke the white line of anger above his mouth. "Otherwise, I'd follow through on my prior intention," he continued with a strained attempt at humor. "But as it is..." Ruefully, he shrugged. "I really do need to get on the road. Would you mind waiting until I pack? Then I'll drop you off on the way."

"No, I don't mind," Eve said, half relieved and half disappointed. "Are you ... Will you be returning?"

"Oh yes, I'll be back, Eve. And you'll be here, waiting for me."

Before she could reply, he pulled her to his chest and kissed her with a trace of the command that had edged his voice.

The tightly contained anger she sensed in him filtered through the hands moving firmly down her back. They cupped the soft rounds of her bottom with no expectation of protest, pressing her to him and holding her there while he kissed her again with the same bold demand.

As before, the blaze of excitement swept through Eve with devastating swiftness. She was lost in his deliciously rough mastery, aflame with the excitement he had taught her to crave. The need to give to him was as primal as breathing. To think that she could stop either natural function seemed totally illogical.

When he took his mouth from hers, she leaned into his strength with a tremulous breath. The depth of her response set off a series of shocks reverberating through her entire body.

Her passion eased into her mind and collided with the words he had spoken. *"You'll be here, waiting for me."*

She drew away from him, but he had clasped his hands behind her back in a light loose embrace, and she could still feel his rapid heartbeat.

"I'll return as soon as possible, Eve," he promised, making her name a caress. "Now come and talk to me while I pack. Maybe you can even give me a hand. I'm lousy at packing."

She didn't give him a hand. Leaning against the door frame, she watched him begin filling a leather valise. "What made you so angry?" she asked.

He shrugged. "You have to know this business."

"All I know is the little you've told me, but I do think I'm intelligent enough to at least get the drift. What did this man do that was so terrible? He's an employee, I suppose?"

"A former employee." Nate walked to his dresser and began stuffing items into his pockets. "I sank every penny I had into this business. So did Patrick. He'd made a considerably smaller investment, but when it's everything you have, size isn't important. We've been lucky, coming in on the ground floor and getting there with the first and the best. But it was still a risky venture. It can take up to eighteen months to design, debug and market a program, and those development costs can be ruinous to a small firm."

He flashed a rueful grin. "I didn't mean to get this involved. To answer your original question, one of our bright young men decided to leave our employ and start his own software firm. He didn't make it. So he started another business. It's called piracy. A trifle illegal, but the initial investment is low. Just run off a few hundred thousand copies of a very fine word-processing program—in this case, mine—and peddle them at cut-rate prices."

A wintry smile hardened his handsome mouth. "Underground, of course. We do have laws against that sort of thing. But you know that old recipe for cooking a goose—first you've got to catch the goose. Well, we caught one. And now—" Nate snapped shut the valise "—we're going to cook it."

"I know what he did was despicable," she argued, "but maybe he was desperate—"

"Or maybe just too lazy to recoup through something called honest labor. He had everything going for him—a fine family, good friends, supportive associates." His tone took on a caustic edge, icily denying the pain she glimpsed in his eyes. "Patrick and I were two of those associate-friends. The emphasis is on 'were.' As far as I'm concerned, friendship doesn't matter a damn when it's based on trickery and deceit."

Tossing down the valise, he put his hands on her shoulders. Eve stared at him in astonishment. Once again the long gray eyes were quicksilver warm and tender.

"I'm sorry, pretty lady. I didn't mean to bore you with all this." Nate tipped her chin for a quick kiss that flowed into something wonderfully wild and passionate. His head swam, and hot prickles of desire savaged his flesh. Suddenly his work didn't matter. Only she did. His voice thickened. "I could delay my departure until morning, Eve."

Angered at her longing—a longing so abject that she shuddered with it—Eve shook her head. "No, don't delay your departure. I can't make love with you, Nate." Her gaze leveled to his. "I want you, you know that. What we have right now is attraction. Elemental chemistry, actually, and that's not much of a reason to tumble into bed."

Elemental chemistry? A gritty laugh raked Nate's throat. He couldn't remember needing a woman so much. "That 'elemental chemistry' has been responsible for more of those 'tumbles' than any other force in existence," he mocked gently. "It could sweep you off your feet and into that bed so fast your head would spin."

"Yes, it could. *You* could," she amended. "A few expert moves on your part and I probably would be in that bed. But I wouldn't feel very good about it in the morning." There came that proud lift of chin he liked so much. "I'm not apologizing, you understand. I'm simply not ready for this."

Weighing her words against the hot-blooded urge to make those few expert moves, Nate let amusement filter through his expression. "Well, we don't want you feeling bad in the morning, so let's get out of here before I forget that. I won't be gone long. Two or three days, tops and I'll be back..." He kissed her nose, his eyes suddenly agleam with sweet arrogance. "And with every intention of changing your mind, Ms. Sheridan!"

Incredible, Eve thought. The man who ushered her out the door bore no resemblance to the cold furious stranger of a few moments ago. But she wasn't likely to forget that stranger, or his ruthless response when someone crossed him.

"So how was your date with the devastating Nate?" Mary Jo asked as soon as Eve came downstairs the next morning.

"Devastating. Coffee, please," she pleaded pitifully. Mary Jo had mercy and fixed her a cup. "He went back to Portland last night," Eve went on. Briefly she explained why. "I hate losing two or three days," she confided, struck by a sense of immediacy. "There's so little time—"

"Oh, nonsense, you have time," Mary Jo rebuked. "You said you had a month's leave if you wanted, so take it. And take it here, while *he's* here."

"Mary Jo, I can't leave Amanda that long! Good grief, I miss her so much already I practically start bawling every time I hang up the phone. You don't know what it's like, being away from your child any significant length of time. They grow so fast, change so fast. She's probably two inches taller and has learned how to turn a somersault, and I didn't get to see it. Don't laugh," she protested. "You don't know how important little things are."

"I suppose not. How do you feel about Nate now?"

"Godiva chocolates. How about Patrick?"

"Sugar cookies." Mary Jo sighed. "But a munchkin like me can't afford *any* kind of cookies."

Tuesday and Wednesday were leaden days, chill and windy with intermittent rain. Mary Jo was closeted in her studio, and Eve moped around the house listlessly. Her mind was evenly divided between thoughts of Nate and her little girl. Amanda's health was not the pressing problem; Eve's housekeeper, a retired nurse, knew how to deal with Amanda's asthma attacks. But Eve missed her child. Their telephone chats, though increasingly frequent, did not alleviate her need to hold and cuddle. Impulsively she decided to drive home.

Although her chief purpose in the visit was to see Amanda, she managed to work in a business meeting with Brian Oliver, who told her she looked fantastic. The sea air, most likely, was responsible. She blushed. He laughed and hugged her, friend-to-friend. Fiercely she hugged him back.

Brian, Mary Jo, Amanda and Eve formed a warm loving circle. Why wasn't it enough for her? Eve wondered.

She used the return drive late Thursday afternoon to ponder that. She'd felt as restless as the wind while she was at home. It's because of Nate, she admitted. Naturally I miss him. He's sexy and exciting—any woman feels more alive when there's an attractive man around. Telling herself this helped diminish the confusion hovering around his image like shifting banks of fog.

With astonishing slowness the mellow afternoon gave way to evening and the sound she'd been waiting for—Nate's foot-steps on the porch. Wondering if her heart could beat this fast without damaging something, she flung open the door. Stand-ing tall and proud, clad in an open-collared shirt and jeans, Nate radiated a magnetic vitality that stole her breath away.

"Hello, pretty lady," he said. And then, without quite knowing how, she was in his arms, clasped tightly to his chest, her face snugged into the curve of his shoulder while his bur-rowed deep into her hair.

"I missed you," he whispered.

"Me, too," she confessed.

Raising his head, Nate said, "I'm hungry. Let's go eat pizza."

"Fine with me," Eve replied. "Let me tell Mary Jo we're leaving first."

Mary Jo was curled up on the studio's cushy windowsill seat, her expression pensive. "Hey, honey," Eve said, ruffling her sooty curls. "You okay?"

"Yes, I'm okay. But I do have something on my mind. Watching you and Nate together, I wondered . . ." Searching dark eyes fixed on Eve's face. "Evie, are you certain you know what you're doing?"

Needing a moment to think, Eve put on her jacket. She felt caught up in a whirlwind when she was with Nate. Well, cer-tain or not, the course of events she'd set in motion would not come to a screeching halt just because she had lost her nerve. Which I haven't, she assured herself.

"I know what I'm doing, honey," she asserted. But suddenly, instinctively, behind her back she crossed her fingers.

Four days later, Eve found herself distracted to the point of absurdity. Blankly she stared at the shoe she held, a scruffy beach clog, when she'd meant to dig out her pumps. Distracted? She was as jumpy as hell. Nate had stayed at the shore only two days before returning to Portland, but he was driving back tonight and would be here the rest of the week.

To her dismay, she found herself dreading the approach of sundown. The thought of another evening alone with him, though undeniably exciting, was also very disturbing. *Because he's ready to get on to the next stage of this relationship, and you, Elizabeth Eve, are not.* "Afraid?" she taunted the shadowed eyes in her mirror.

Pride promptly rejected that possibility. Actually, she had several very good reasons for stalling. She was pondering her behavior dressed only in a shower cap, and one of those reasons was disturbingly apparent. Tiny white lines marred the pale gold skin of her lower abdomen. The stretch marks of childbirth, and Nate had no idea she had a child.

Telling him was bound to be awkward; she'd waited long past the point where such confidences were normal. But the thought of sharing her child with Nate, in any way, filled her with a smothering sense of panic.

"Which is stupid in itself," she muttered, slapping a svelte thigh in smarting rebuke. She wasn't an emotional cripple. Just sensibly cautious. Any woman in her position would be.

Relieved at such practical reasoning, she decided not to dig any deeper. No telling what I might discover down there, she thought with a pinch of humor.

Still, she ought to at least *mention* her child's existence. But Amanda was so precious to her. And if anything went wrong...it didn't bear thinking about. Snatching off the shower cap, she began dressing. Nothing would go wrong. How could it?

"All I'm going to do is tell him, very casually, that I have a child," she informed her cousin, who'd come in needing help with a stuck zipper.

"About time, I'd say," was Mary Jo's succinct opinion. Zipped up, she left in a dithery rush for her own social affair.

Chuckling, Eve turned back to the mirror. The slender navy blouson frock she'd chosen featured an elasticized band across her bosom and wrist-length sleeves edged with antique ecru lace. A short, woven gold band encircled her throat. Her hair was up, and fine sprays of gold danced at her ears. Suede pumps accentuated her legs and added another three inches to her bravado. She looked strong, sophisticated. Then she answered the door and discovered she had wet noodles for muscles.

Imposingly tall and handsome, Nate folded his arms across his chest and looked her up and down. "Gorgeous," he decided.

"So are you," she returned the compliment tartly. He wore an impeccably tailored suit. How could a man resemble an untamed tiger in a black formal suit? she wondered. "You want to come in?"

"No, it's nearly time..." Nate paused, suddenly aware of the song in his heart. A song that had been missing for what seemed an eon of deep inner loneliness, which had been replaced by her smile.

Unable to sustain such romanticism, he cocked his head. "Is that all there is to the top of that dress? Not that I'm complaining, mind you. I just wondered if I ought to carry a stick."

In feminine reaction, Eve spread her fingers over the expanse of naked skin between her throat and the upper swells of her breasts. She had worn the dress on other dates, with other men. But never had she felt so desirable, so seductively female as when she wore it for Nate.

She held her breath as their eyes locked in intimate communion.

His breath came in a soft hiss of surprise.

A new element entered their relationship so stealthily it startled them both. Something gut-deep and earthy stripped away their formality and changed even the quality of their thoughts.

Nate's next act confirmed her intuitive awareness. He had never used coarse language with her, but what came out of the mouth nuzzling her ear was teasingly erotic.

Disconcerted, she looked at him with childlike seriousness, then broke into a laugh.

Nate laughed with her, his mood lusty and buoyant as he escorted her to the car. Her demure aura had been replaced by a radiant sexuality that hit him like a joyous blow. With each successive evening they spent together, Eve seemed to unfold a little more, first the tight bud he had met on the beach, and now this nearly bloomed flower. What would she be like when she fully trusted and relaxed with him?

She was stretching her arms above her head, throwing into bold relief the piquant points of her breasts. His hands itched. "Eve," he groaned. Her eyes widened. "Will you stop that wiggling about and sit still?"

"Well, I am sitting on a hump, you know," she shot back. "And this center seat belt is digging into my back. Maybe I'll just move over to my side of the car."

"You stay right where you are," he squelched that stupid idea. "Besides, don't you know pain builds character?"

When she heard those words, Eve was taken with a peculiar fit of mirth. He didn't know what was so funny, but listening to her laughter was similar to being bathed in champagne bubbles. The sweet, slow burn of desire was even more enthralling when coupled with the intense satisfaction of being with her.

For Eve, the laughter was a release that blunted caution and created a time warp of pleasure. The atmosphere of a darkened car was tailor-made for the joyous, almost innocent sexuality vibrating between them.

In the chandeliered elegance of the restaurant, each lingering touch magnified what his eyes were saying. He was a virile man, and she was the most beautiful woman in the room. For him, she was the *only* woman in the room.

After dinner they danced to the slow, seductive strains of music she didn't hear, to a beat that throbbed through her blood instead of her feet. It was a romantic evening, and she felt voluptuously female.

Perversely, when they left the club, her effervescent mood reversed so swiftly that the drive back to his house for a nightcap seemed much longer than usual. How ironic, she reflected as they entered his den. She had drifted carelessly into that exquisite time warp, letting herself be carried along on its delicious tide of pleasure without thought of past or future. Now, thrust back into reality, she felt as uncomfortable as a teenager.

"Would you like some wine?" he asked. Relaxed and at ease, he walked to the bar discarding his jacket and tie along the way. The vivid gleam in his eyes left no doubt as to how he expected the evening to end.

Tongue-tied, she shook her head, then flushed at his quizzical arch of brow. Oh God, she thought, I'm acting like an idiot. "Maybe I will have that glass of wine, after all," she said, stalling for time.

There was no more time.

"Later," he whispered. After kissing the frantically beating pulse in her throat, he let his lips graze downward to the edge of her neckline.

Logic told her if she meant to stop this, she had better do it now. But logic was useless tonight. Mesmerized, Eve watched his long fingers gather the soft fabric of her dress and peel it down to her waist.

She heard the sharp intake of his breath as he stepped back to look at her. Seen through the black lace bra, her breasts were small but lush and ripely full. He took down her hair and spread it over her naked shoulders with a look of wonder at the privilege. The shimmering gold strands lay like autumn sunlight against her skin, parting around her rosy nipples, converging again to completely cover her breasts. The velvety caress of his voice roused them to firm peaks before he ever touched them.

She didn't hear what he said. Words were meaningless garble in the glow of his eyes. Her skin heated. Thrill after erotic thrill twisted through her nerve endings. The silky pressure of his lips skimming along the contours of her throat filled her lungs with air that was not enough, never enough. Passion was a warm obliterating blanket fusing her to his rock-hard thighs.

She had to get closer, closer still. Nothing existed but this hot, demanding urgency.

Somehow she was on the couch, her body pressed deep into its cushiony surface, his weight a descending burden she welcomed with mindless craving.

"Eve, I want you so. I couldn't stand it if you didn't want me." His whisper was thick and fervid. His mouth ravished hers, his tongue penetrating with a sexual rhythm.

Out of control. The warning careened around the edges of her mind. But it was too weak to pierce the sensuous haze of desire.

It was Nate who stopped them.

Bracing himself above her, he whispered, "I don't want our first time together to be like this—on a couch, fully clothed. I'm sorry, honey," he said deeply. "I nearly lost control, very nearly made a mess out of this." He gave her a crooked grin. "But you're so tempting, Eve." His fingers trembled as he touched her skin. "Flawless!" he marveled.

Rising, he held out his hands to her. "Let's do this right," he said huskily.

"Don't, Nate!" She twisted, evading his reach. "I don't want to do this right. I don't want to do it at all!" she blurted.

Nate dropped his hands and slowly straightened. Along with other emotions storming his mind and body, he felt foolish.

It was not a feeling he could tolerate for long, not with his towering pride. Not with *this* woman. "Why not, Eve?"

Hurriedly she sat up and covered herself, then smoothed her disordered hair. He sat down beside her, his gaze probing her flushed face. "I asked you why not."

Confused, with no time to be confused, Eve shut her eyes. "I'm sorry, Nate," she said dully. "You weren't the only one who lost control." She winced, remembering the abandon with which she'd fallen into his arms, her wild craving to know again, at any cost, the fiery ecstasy of his loving. "But there is a good reason why not." Her smile was a tremulous offering. "Two good reasons, actually."

Expressionless, he studied her. His voice, when he spoke, was cool and gentle. "What are those reasons, Eve?"

"Well, for one thing," she said with supremely feminine reasoning, "I am not flawless. Not below the waist, at any rate. I don't have much of a tan, but that wouldn't matter. Stretch marks rarely tan. They're from childbirth. Nate, I have a daughter."

Five

Moving without his usual grace, Nate stared at Eve. His eyes were dark, his expression inscrutable.

"I see," he said finally. "That's quite an omission, Eve. We've known each other for more than two weeks, and with all the hours we've spent together, that's equivalent to months of dating. Yet you never got around to telling me something as important as this," he marveled. He folded his arms across his chest. "You want to tell me why?"

"Because it's such a highly personal thing, that's why," Eve snapped defensively.

"Funny." His cold, speculative gaze roamed her set face. "I thought we had reached and even passed the 'highly personal' stage of this baffling relationship."

"We had—have—but I... Nate, please, Amanda is the most important thing in my life. She *is* my life. And it isn't easy to bare such intimate confidences to a stranger."

He flinched at that word. "We're not strangers, Eve. From the moment we met, I knew you," he rebuked, stopping her heart with a convulsive jolt of shock. "Sometimes it can be that way, you know. No rhyme or reason for it, but I felt it immediately. I think you did, too.''

"Oh yes, I felt it," Eve agreed with fine irony. She folded her hands and sat up straight, ankles crossed. "I'm sorry, Nate, I should have told you about Amanda."

"I won't argue with that." Grudgingly appeased, he strode to the bar and uncapped a crystal decanter. "How old is she?"

Eve hesitated as the memory of a ruthlessly capable man suddenly shot to mind. She didn't reason, she just reacted. "Just turned three," she said, although Amanda was seven months older.

"And her father?" He rapped out the question, his chest constricting as images flooded his mind. He snapped his fingers, a sharp sound. "Oh course, that high school sweetheart of yours."

Ignoring the nerves jumping wildly in her stomach, Eve decided to neither deny nor confirm his assumption that that relationship had produced her child. "Nate, I really don't want to get into this any deeper," she began.

But he was already into his next question. "He didn't want the baby?" Nate handed her a glass of sherry.

She sipped it. "Obviously not. Amanda's father didn't need either me or my baby. And after the initial shock wore off, I realized my child and I didn't need him. So it all evens out. I have Amanda entirely to myself, and he has no idea what he's lost."

Such brave defiance, Nate thought. His voice gentled. "Amanda. That's a lovely name. Your mother's?"

"My grandmother's."

"And who does Amanda resemble? Her mother, I hope?"

"Some. She's beautiful, of course...."

His quick grin evoked a blush.

"She looks like..." *Like you and me, the best of our features.* "Like a mischievous elf! So tiny and fragile...and so sturdy, so incredibly energetic. She has my eyes, but her hair comes from my mother. Silvery blond, almost a true platinum, and marvelously thick and curly."

"She does sound beautiful. But I'm not surprised. Am I going to meet her?"

"I don't know," she said distractedly. "I was planning to take her to the mountains after I leave here, but maybe the beach... I know I've certainly enjoyed being here. We didn't spend much time on beaches when I was a child. Mother didn't like them—the sand, the hippies. Beaches were nasty places, she said." She paused for a breath. "I'm sorry, I'm babbling and I know it."

"You are, but I'm enjoying it. Mother didn't like hippies, hmm? How did Mother feel about Amanda?"

His easy tone nettled her. Rising, she walked to the bar and set down her glass with a sharp click. "We had a rather violent confrontation when I told her I was pregnant, and I went to live in Concord. I didn't see her again until... until the day she suffered a massive stroke. She died that night without ever regaining consciousness."

"You mean she never saw her granddaughter at all?"

Nate's quietly incredulous question increased her irritation. "No, she never saw her granddaughter. I told you we disagreed violently, and I meant just that."

"Why?"

"Because she wanted me to go away and have the baby, give it up for adoption, and no one would be the wiser." Realizing that Nate was watching her in the bar's mirror, Eve straightened. "Don't get the wrong idea. Mother wasn't deliberately cruel or unkind—or even coldhearted, for that matter. After the funeral I went up to the attic, and there were my baby clothes, my toys and my dolls, all carefully stowed away for her grandchildren. So pathetic, such a waste of love...."

Her eyes were shiny with the tears she would not permit. "She was my *mother*, dammit! I never knew what that meant until I had Amanda. And then I didn't know how to bridge the gap between us. Like a child, I kept waiting for her to make the first move. But she didn't."

Nate walked up behind her and wrapped her in his arms. "Maybe she couldn't. Sometimes people make a prison for themselves, and they can't break free of it even though they want to desperately." He kissed her neck. "I think you had a raw deal all the way around, and I'm sorry for that, too."

His words rankled. How dare he offer her pity! "I don't feel that way, not at all," she said curtly. "I had a stab at fulfilling a dream, I experienced the wonder of love, I had a baby. All rich and fulfilling experiences many women never know. Why on earth should I think I got a raw deal?"

"I'm sorry. Evidently I was wrong there, too."

The dark, almost comical irony of her situation struck home with enough force to moderate her wrath. "Well, there was a time when I thought differently," she confessed. "No one in the world could have felt sorrier for Eve Sheridan than Eve Sheridan. But that ended about two minutes after they placed Amanda in my arms." Exasperation tinged her quick laugh. "Enough, already! Let's change the subject, okay?"

"For now," he agreed. His embrace tightened until she was pressed against the powerful contours of his body.

Her anger ignited again at the ache that began throbbing in the pit of her stomach. "Stop it!" she snapped.

His soft laugh held a hint of impatience. "Eve, I don't understand all these 'stops' and 'don'ts.' I haven't rushed you, I sensed that you'd been hurt, and I *do* realize how very much you have been hurt." His tone roughened as her body tried to ignore his caress. "But that's the past—this is us. And I don't consider this the usual beach affair. Had I done so, I'd never have tolerated that on-again, off-again signal you kept sending me."

A husky chuckle stirred her hair. "But I knew you were worth the torment, I knew without a doubt what a marvelously beautiful experience making love would be. For both of us, honey. So tell me, my lovely torment," he murmured, "what's stopping us from enjoying something we both want and need?"

Responsive only to the explosive pressure ballooning in her chest, Eve twisted out of his arms. "Everything, that's what! It *was* just a meaningless affair," she flung at him, confusing past with present. "And after it's over, after you've *enjoyed*, you can run back to your familiar haunts and forget you ever met a girl named Eve!"

He cupped her face, his indulgent, comprehending smile intolerably gentle. "Oh Eve, don't tar me with another man's guilt. I could never forget you—"

"Couldn't you?" She wrenched her face aside with a contemptuous laugh, struggling to contain the words tearing at her throat, knowing, to her horror, that she could not. "Well, I wasn't so unforgettable when we spent that 'marvelously beautiful' weekend together!"

Nate went rigid. "We've met before?" His voice rose and cracked with disbelief. "And spent a weekend together?"

Dumbly, Eve nodded.

"By 'together' you mean we—"

"Slept together, made love, had sex—whatever you want to call it," Eve cut in, her voice shaking with the shock of her savage outburst. Acknowledging her stupidity wasn't the worst of it. She still had to defuse the situation. Somehow.

Stepping back, he asked flatly, "When? And where?"

Eve stared at a spot just beyond his shoulder.

"In Las Vegas. You came into the club where I worked—a small place off the Strip—and after my performance, you slipped me a note asking me to have dinner with you."

A glance into his opaque gray eyes increased her anxiety. They were probing her face, seeming to analyze it with his scrutiny. Diverting her gaze, she plowed on, "I rarely dated back then, but you seemed nice, courteous, different from the usual run of men and I . . . said yes."

"When was that?" he asked tersely, his throat tightening as shocked disbelief swirled into crazily mixed emotions.

"Several years ago," she replied, looking up as she spoke. The gaze fixed on her face was blank, his expression abstracted, as if he were searching for something inside himself. "You really don't remember, do you?" Her unemotional voice made it a statement rather than a question. A smile of sorts tilted her lips. "Oh well, who can blame you? All those years, so many affairs. Can't expect a man to keep track of them all, I suppose."

Except for the wince around his eyes, Nate ignored her gibe.

"When, exactly?" he sliced through her deliberate vagueness.

Her neck bent like the stem of a fragile flower under a heavy rain. "I told you, several years ago. Who remembers? Certainly not you. Strange, isn't it? How every woman holds on to the fond illusion that she's different, unique in some small way." Her mouth went awry. "Unforgettable."

"Yes, dammit, unforgettable! Unless something..." Nate paused, stunned and incredulous. It couldn't be! Or could it? "It was around four—four and a half years ago, wasn't it? *Wasn't it?*" he demanded, his eyes blazing with excitement as it all came together like a clash of cymbals.

He answered himself before she could. "Yes, it was. My God," he whispered, wonderingly. He had never regained his memory of that lost weekend. Even the fact that it had happened was eventually forgotten. Having convinced himself that nothing significant had occurred, he had let it sink beneath his subconscious to surface now and then as a soft aching sadness that seemed to exist for no reason at all.

But there was a reason! "You!" He strode across the room and pulled her up, then cradled her face in his hands. "It was *you!*"

Eve could hardly draw breath, much less stand. She grabbed his shoulders. "You remember?"

Those lovely purple eyes were wide open to him. Nate's mind reeled under the sudden assault of guilt and contrition. Thank heaven he had an explanation.

"No, Eve, I don't remember—but I do, and that's—God, that's wonderful!" he exulted, and started planting kisses all over the most baffled face he'd ever had the privilege to look upon.

"Nate, either you do or you don't," she said crossly. "Which is it?"

"Both! It was the accident," he said, explaining nothing that she could see. "Amnesia, Eve. Oh, I know how clichéd that sounds, but it does happen," he answered her skeptical look. "I'd just got home from Vegas..." In a tumbling rush of words, he related his accident and its aftereffects. "Patrick filled me in on most of my lost week, but he wasn't with me in Vegas, so—" Nate spread his hands "—I never knew. Until now."

"Amnesia." Eve whispered. She sank into a chair, feeling light-headed at knowing he had valid cause for his lack of recall. "So you went to Vegas to have a little fun."

"No, it wasn't just to 'have a little fun,'" he mimicked angrily. "At the time I had just come through a divorce, my personal life was a shambles, my work schedule incredible. I had to have some form of release."

"So that's what I was," she murmured. "A form of release."

"I doubt it, but in all honesty, I don't know." Nate's tone was clipped and defensive. Although exonerated, guilt still nibbled at him. "I do know I had some odd feelings when I thought about it later, in the hospital. But I never could figure out if they stemmed from the weekend or just the mess I'd made of my life."

His tone roughened. "I didn't want the divorce—I loved my wife. I also neglected her, but I stupidly considered that to be the price we both had to pay for success. We were perfecting the Starrmark One, readying it for mass production. Dammit, I was *busy*! I expected her to be patient, to wait until I did have time for her. But she got tired of waiting." Savagely Nate raked through his hair. "Eight years of marriage down the drain, and there wasn't a damn thing I could do about it. I was totally powerless."

"I know the feeling," Eve said dryly.

"Then you also know how wild and crazy you can get." He laughed without mirth. "I kept having visions of a padded cell."

"Well, I wasn't quite that bad."

"Bad enough, though," Nate said, his tone hardening again. "Did he ever see the baby?"

Caught off guard, Eve sipped her wine, her mind flying from one approach to another. She still couldn't think straight, but instinct warned her that words had become dangerous, and she heeded her instincts. Although not infallible, they were certainly more reliable than a disorganized brain.

"No. He moved away soon after we broke up. I never saw him again." She stood up. "I'd like to go home now, please."

"First I've got a question that needs answering." Gray eyes bored into hers. "Was our meeting here coincidence?"

"Sheer coincidence. I was stunned when I first saw you."

"Why didn't you say something?"

"That's two questions. Anyway, what was I supposed to say? 'Hey, remember me, one of your old bed partners?' " She grabbed her purse and wrap and walked to the door.

Nate followed without protest. He was preoccupied on the drive home, and Eve kept her silence. She had accepted his explanation, even empathized with the pain that had shown in his eyes, but there was still the matter of how their affair ended.

She hadn't forgotten the humiliation of his indulgent dismissal. She hadn't forgotten anything.

"You said there were two reasons why you couldn't make love with me," he said as he pulled into her driveway. "What's the other one?"

"I won't be swept off my feet into something I'm still not sure about." She glanced at his strong profile. "You respect that?"

"Yes."

No qualifiers. With an approving nod, she opened the door. "Don't bother getting out. We're both too beat for long good nights." Before he could respond, she was out of the car and running up the steps.

By the time his taillights disappeared, she was sitting on her bedroom balcony wrapped in a spare blanket, staring blindly at the ocean. Fatigue dragged at her eyelids, but she was too agitated to sleep. Tonight had been a jarring shock to her preconceptions. Thinking herself well prepared, she'd found she was prepared for nothing, including the eruption of caustic resentment that resulted in her dangerous outburst.

Where had it come from? And why hadn't she been able to contain it?

And did she dare carry out the next test she'd planned for Nate—an introduction to his daughter? Of course he wouldn't know Amanda was his. Still, it was risky, especially now that he knew about Vegas. But he had no idea he was a father. How could he possibly guess? And she had to see how he interacted with a child. Why, he might not even like children!

Her embattled brain refused to function beyond this point. Wearily Eve went back inside. She would think about it tomorrow.

Tomorrow was too far off for Nate to postpone his painful reflections. He felt too keyed up to go to bed and strangely averse to probing through the surprises Eve had sprung on him.

Something tugged at his mind, an uneasiness, as if he had missed some vital point in their discussion.

He shoved that problem aside. His disciplined mind was well schooled in subconsciously separating the wheat from the chaff. Sooner or later, a resolution usually presented itself. But he had a suspicion that this time the mind he was so justly proud of had met its match. Although he could not figure out why, Eve was more of a riddle than ever.

Thoughts of the faceless man who'd fathered her child twisted his gut. Hurriedly he skipped over that. He wished he'd told her more about the emotional mess he'd been after the divorce. Maybe she'd have reciprocated. But he'd never been much good at communicating his private feelings, even with Barbara. After their divorce, he found it nearly impossible to open all those locked doors.

Abandoning this unproductive line of thought, he poured some cognac while mulling through Eve's revelations. At least he now knew why he'd felt that sense of immediate recognition. Come to think of it, he also knew why she turned maddeningly cool and aloof just when they were closest.

On the practical side, he wasn't much bothered by her new status. He'd casually dated several women who had children, keeping it light because he didn't want to get involved. So where did that leave Eve? And him? His soft smile supplied the answer: wanting her as much as ever, and respecting her all the more.

His idle reflections had somewhat settled his mind but had not soothed his body. Rain, accompanied by the soft plaintive sigh of wind and rustling leaves, whispered up erotic images. Desire came, quick and urgent. Eve. How the devil he could have forgotten making love to her was a masculine mystery. The feel and taste of her, the way she smelled... Odd how her scent still filled his nostrils. An evocative fragrance composed of expensive perfume on warm feminine flesh....

Irritably he tossed down his drink. He had a fire in his loins and a telephone within arm's distance. But he didn't want another woman. He wanted Eve. Tempting, unpredictable, lovely Eve. The kind of woman designed to drive a man crazy, he thought as the flames of his desire burned brighter. But a very special woman, nonetheless.

The following morning, Eve was awakened by Mary Jo's exasperated voice demanding she get up immediately; there was a crazy man in her living room.

"What? Who?" Eve asked most lucidly.

"A crazy man, I said," Mary Jo whispered. "Will you for God's sake get up and go do something with him? And remind him it's only eight o'clock and that I happened to have been *sleeping*?" she requested with another rude shake.

The latter was unnecessary; Eve was wide awake. Speeding to the dresser, she raked a brush through her hair and grabbed up a robe. She had one arm in it when she reached the living room. Mary Jo's madman stood just inside the door, his gray eyes very nearly hidden behind a mountain of flowers.

"What on earth!" Eve gasped.

"Good morning!" Nate said. "You want to take these things? I think I'm going to sneeze."

Eve finished putting on her robe and hastily belted it. Her heart was beating double time. "Where did you get flowers this hour of the morning?" she asked helplessly as both her arms were overfilled with blossoms. "And why, come to think of it?"

"Our local florist is a friend of mine. He was delighted to open his shop an hour or two early, especially for such a good cause. Did anyone ever tell you you're beautiful? These flowers pale in comparison. Why don't you lay them on the couch," he suggested, "and then come here."

Dumping them on the couch, Eve approached him with visible suspicion. Was he drunk? Or was he just crazy, as Mary Jo claimed? "I think I asked why," she remembered.

Nate's warm hands settled on her shoulders. "Because I started thinking how I'd feel if I met up with a woman I'd known intimately, and she didn't remember me, and I confess I didn't like the thought of not being recognized, regardless of the reason. I am sorry, Eve, but I don't know what I can do about it. Except offer flowers and a sincere apology."

Impatience concealed the lump in her throat. "Oh Nate, for heaven's sake, you didn't have to go to all this trouble. My hurt feelings probably stemmed more from vanity than anything else."

"You didn't feel that way last night," Nate countered. "I saw how you looked at me when you first started talking. I'm still not certain of exactly what I did see, but it sure as hell wasn't a fond memory of a nice, courteous man."

"Well, maybe I did get a little hot about it," Eve admitted. "But that incredible mass of flowers and your sincere apology has soothed the scratches, so let's forget about it, okay?"

"If that's what you want. Look, the reason I'm here so early is that I need to get back to the office. I won't be gone long. In fact," he said, looking thoughtful, "I could be lured back tonight if I knew there would be someone waiting for me at my house with a fantastic meal and a sweet smile."

"A meal *I'm* to cook?"

"The way to a man's heart," he reminded.

"Forget it," she said shortly. "I'm not interested."

Surprised by her spontaneous flare of temper and too stubborn to back down, Eve turned from him. She'd barely taken a step before he spun her around to face him.

Nate's tight grip and angry face made her eyes widen. "Don't give me that," he ground out. "You *are* interested. You know it and I know it. Because of you I got about an hour's sleep last night—"

"Well, I didn't get all that much sleep, either! But if a home-cooked meal means that much to you, then all right, blast it, I'll do it!" She glared at him, seeing the humor in her furious rebuttal reflected in his twitch of lips.

"Well! That's better," he said, mollified.

"Then stop bruising me. Dinner's at seven. Don't be late," she said sternly.

"Not a chance, lady!" He hesitated, looking oddly young and unsure. "Did I bother to mention that I think I've met a very wonderful woman? Her name is Eve. Bye, honey. See you at seven." Brushing a kiss upon her open mouth, he left.

The sound of his car faded away, and still Eve made no move to gather up his flowers. Mary Jo's sour voice startled her. "Well, let's get these things off the couch. Luckily the pantry has a plentiful supply of vases."

In the kitchen, cramming in handfuls of blossoms with little regard to style, Mary Jo said hesitantly, "Eve, I didn't mean to eavesdrop—well, actually, I did mean to eavesdrop—but I'm dying of curiosity. I'm sorry I wasn't here when you came in last night. I wanted to hear about his reaction to Amanda. Instead I was standing around a crowded art gallery, forced to mingle and smile and socialize until my teeth hurt."

Wanly, Eve smiled. "Dull, huh?"

"'Dull' does not suffice. Try intellectual claustrophobia. But one does have to nurture one's contacts, so sayeth my agent."

Mary Jo left off flower stuffing and poured two cups of coffee. "So tell me, how did he react?"

Eve stuck six pink roses into a pewter vase and admired the results before saying slowly, "Angrily at first, which was natural. Then tenderly. I think he's really the nice guy he seems to be, Mary Jo."

"I wouldn't be a bit surprised," Mary Jo declared. "I told you I liked him, and I never like unnice people. Getting back to eavesdropping, would this avalanche of flowers and that sincere apology relate to his forgetting your Vegas weekend, by any chance? I thought you weren't going to mention that," she said in response to Eve's nod. "What happened? Lose your cool?"

"A monumental understatement, but yes, I lost my cool."

Tersely she recounted last night's events, including Nate's accident.

"Amnesia!" Wide-eyed, Mary Jo considered the validity of that, then decided in his favor. "I knew he'd have a good excuse. But what's so horrid about letting him think that what's-his-name is Amanda's father? If he knew about Vegas, then you couldn't very well tell him you came home pregnant. On the

other hand, you said he's a nice guy, so what if he did put two
and two together and came up with Amanda? Basically you'd
have what you wanted, a father to help raise her.''

"Maybe I don't want any help raising her! Darn it, Mary Jo,
I've had her all to myself ever since she was born, and I don't
like the thought of sharing her, having someone else telling her
what we can and cannot do. That's *my* job, *my* privilege." Eve
pursed her lips as she weighed her own words. Catching her
cousin's eyes, she spread her hands in a gesture of confusion.
"It seemed so simple when I started this."

"Nothing's ever simple where a man is concerned." Mary Jo
grunted. "Well, I've got work to do. Grab the coffeepot and tag
along. We'll continue this upstairs."

Agreeably Eve followed her to the airy pine-floored study
that served as her studio. Stark white walls made a stunning
frame for the canvases hung or propped against them.

"This is still my favorite," Eve said, pausing before a sweetly
familiar seascape. The huge granite boulder stood like a senti-
nel against an angry sea. The sweep of sky and water subtly
lightened to a tender wash of blue, and the luminous ruffle that
separated sea and sand might have been mist or merely imagination. In the velvety medley of grays, an iridescent lavender
and pink seashell had the joyous effect of a shout of laughter.

"Every time I look at it, I see something different," she
murmured. "That raging sea, so dark and threatening, and the
boulder, holding back the night. And then that soft faint
promise of tomorrow's sunshine... It's beautiful, Mary Jo."

"You have very good taste," Mary Jo proclaimed. "I could
have sold that thing a dozen times over, but I like it too much
to part with it for mere money. By the way, I've got some good
news. Terrific, actually!" Opening her voluminous handbag,
she withdrew a glossy magazine. "Remember that interview I
did for that art magazine? Well they decided to use it for a fea-
ture-length article, and here it is!" she crowed, waving it under Eve's nose. "Oh Eve, do you realize what this kind of
exposure means to the proverbial starving artist? My agent
called yesterday. She's already getting some interest from col-
lectors. Is a Mary J. a good investment? Heck yes, it is!"

"Oh honey, that's wonderful!" Eve breathed. "One thing, though, Ms. Mary Collectible J. If you ever do decide to sell that seascape, remember, it's mine. Even if I have to hock my car to buy it!"

"You can't buy it, but you might get it as a wedding present. That should give you an incentive to cook up an extra special feast tonight!"

Eve stiffened. "Let's cut out the wedding talk, shall we? Sensitive subject," she explained.

"I'm sorry, I wasn't thinking." Dark eyes slanted. "By the way, what *are* you cooking up tonight?"

The rosy flush of heat reached Eve's cheeks before she replied, slowly, and with a hint of sensuous mischief in her eyes, "I've been wondering about that myself, Mary Jo."

Six

Eve loved to cook, and Nate's sleek stainless-steel and shining-tile kitchen was a joy to work in. Humming a tuneless air, she prepared a tray of hors d'oeuvres and carried them to the spacious den.

Set against the lowering night, masses of fresh flowers, soft music and a crackling fire created an idyllic scene. "Perfect!" she exulted. Then the telephone rang.

"I'm sorry, Eve, but I've gotten tied up and I don't know when I can get away," Nate said, apologetic and brusque. "An important employee experienced some severe chest pains this evening, and I can't leave until I know if it's really indigestion as he claimed, or something more serious. I am sorry. I know you've gone to a lot of trouble, but ... you do understand?"

Compassion softened her disappointment. "Yes, of course I understand. I'll wait for you, if you want, Nate."

"Thanks, honey, but I couldn't ask you to do that. No telling what time I'll be in. They're doing tests right now and we—his wife and I—are waiting for the results. It could be after eleven before I get home."

The strain in his naturally deep voice pierced her heart and formed what seemed a perfectly natural decision. "That doesn't matter. I have a lovely fire going, and I'll just cuddle up and watch TV or something. And if I get sleepy, I'll go to sleep."

"In my bed?" Quickly he laughed. "Sorry, that was out of line. I spoke before I thought.... But it was such a *lovely* thought." He sighed. "I'll be there as soon as I can. By the way, what *was* dinner?"

Beef Stroganoff, she told him. His favorite, he promptly announced. She laughed. "It'll keep. So will I. See you when you get here."

"Another lovely thought," he murmured. "But just in case you change your mind, leave a light burning for me?"

"If I change my mind," Eve agreed. After cleaning the kitchen, she sat down in his recliner, feeling curiously content to be in this lovely room even though she was alone. Sipping an apricot brandy before a cheery fire was a sensuous pleasure, she discovered.

For a time she mulled over her decision to bring Amanda to the beach house, a decision that made her stomach churn every time she thought of it. But she'd spent too many hours agonizing over that already. Besides, blurring the child's age had killed any suspicion Nate might have about her father. So stop worrying, she chided herself.

By midnight Eve was yawning repeatedly, feeling pleasantly relaxed and drowsy. Idly she considered going home. Nate wouldn't expect her to wait this late. But she didn't want to go home. The blood flowing through her veins was enriched by brandy, and its lovely, tingly warmth had pooled at the base of her stomach. She wasn't thinking, she was simply feeling. And what she felt was the anticipation of a woman waiting for her man to come home.

Waiting for him in his bed. The thought was wildly alluring. Just envisioning his reaction sent tiny shocks of erotic delight down her spine. Uncontrollably, she shivered, remembering how his eyes had glowed the first time he'd gazed upon her naked form. Their brilliance had been like a magnet, exerting a force that drew her ever deeper into the whirlwind they rode through a night that was like no other. Ever. And afterward, the euphoric sense of completeness she had never known again....

Contemplating the hot red glow of embers, all that remained of her lovely apple-wood fire, Eve wasn't aware of making any conscious decisions. She was suddenly tired of denying her feminine needs. She was every bit as much a woman as he was a man, just as hungry for intimacy. As if she'd pulled a plug, more memories welled up from the depths, making her body burn for the touch of his hard male flesh and seeking hands.

Shaken by fiery longing, she uttered a soft protest. She still wasn't sure if she was ready for the emotional complexities of lovemaking. But she wanted him. She wanted to be under him, to feel again the delicious heaviness of him sinking into her yielding softness, easing this intense, angry aching that gripped her like sensual talons.

It was her choice.

Coming swiftly to her feet, Eve strode to his bedroom.

Here the decorator had created an aura as impersonal as a luxurious hotel suite, yet Nate had left his imprint. He always would, she thought proudly. No matter where he chose to lay his head, the magnetic vitality that was Nate incarnate would always leave its mark.

In the bathroom, traces of his spicy after-shave hung in the air like a forceful presence. Quickly she undressed and bathed, wishing she had some perfume; glad, on second thought, that she did not. The scent of Eve would be all that clung to his skin when she left him.

She brushed out her hair until it shimmered. Hands trembling, she turned back the bed's puffy coverlet to discover satin sheets. They felt wonderfully cool on her hot skin. Turning onto her side in a flow of lissome curves, she closed her eyes. Within minutes she was drifting into a silken drowse.

Nate came in around one. Hurriedly he unlocked the door, hoping she would be there, warning himself that she probably would not. Although his shoulders slumped, he smiled as he noted the light she'd left burning for him. The air still smelled of the meal she had prepared, and woven through its fragrance like a line of some exquisite melody, was her perfume.

He sat down on the couch and discarded his shoes and socks. Then he balled up his shirt and flung it aside. Clicking off the lamp, he leaned against the couch in weary contemplation of another restless night.

It was then that he noticed the thin ray of light straying down the hall from his bedroom.

The heady jolt of excitement froze him for an instant. Then he was following the beckoning finger of light with all the joyous eagerness of a man coming home from a long cold journey.

She was asleep, one arm flung over her head, her hair a spun-gold mist fanning across the hyacinth-blue pillowcase. Warm and soft and naked in his bed, just as he had imagined.... Becoming aware of his moonstruck behavior, he roused himself, overwhelmed by the rage of desire pounding in his blood. He had wanted many women and taken his pleasure with some of them, but what Eve aroused within him defied description.

He leaned over her and brushed his lips across the satiny curve of her cheek, inhaling her sweetness until his head spun.

She stirred. "Nate," she whispered, touching his cheek.

"Hello, Eve," he said deeply. Then the breath went out of him. Still half-asleep, she looked up at him with eyes nearly veiled by those incredible lashes, and he saw the strange expression that never failed to mystify him.

"Your friend—is he all right?" she remembered.

"He's fine. He'll be released in the morning. It was severe heartburn brought on by severe pigging out. Which he'll think twice about doing again. I told him I'd kill him if he ever gave me another scare like that.... Good Lord, I'm babbling like an idiot."

"So you are," she observed. "Any particular reason?"

His knees buckled. Sinking down beside her, he stroked her hair, saying gruffly, "Yes. You. I wanted this so, and yet I didn't dare let myself hope that you'd even be waiting for me." His knuckles grazed her cheek. The tenderness of his touch belied the rugged strength of his hands.

He was never more aware of that strength. The need to be
gentle, to protect and cherish, rose up like a fierce white heat.

"Eve." He spoke quietly. "Are you sure you want this?"

"I'm sure, Nate. At this moment, that's about all I'm sure
of."

"But is it enough?"

"It's enough." Like delicate butterflies, her hands drifted to
his shoulders. "Don't talk," she requested softly. "Just make
love to me."

His next words were spoken on her lips. "That, my lovely
Eve, is something I intend doing for the rest of this long, dark
night."

Desire hazed her eyes as she watched him undress. The lean
body rising nakedly from its clutter of clothes was wondrously
familiar. She felt a flush of almost liquid warmth.

She held out her arms, and he slid into them. Her soft, silken
nudity restored the heat to his night-chilled skin. Like tiny
daggers, her fingernails trailed down his back to tight-muscled
buttocks, creating rich, shuddery excitement as tinder to feed
the flames.

When he propped himself up on one elbow and drew back
the sheet, she made no move to conceal herself from his
scorching gaze. Although he was burning with desire, he took
time to savor this visual feast. Where the sun didn't touch, her
skin was the luminous color of a pearl. The white network of
stretch marks she considered so unsightly merely led his gaze to
the bewitching golden triangle lying in the pale valley of her
thighs. Erect pink nipples and the navel dimpling the slight
curve of her belly enticed his lips. Again and again, like a man
sipping nectar from some exotic chalice, he dipped his mouth
to her while she received the mist of kisses with shuddery little
breaths.

He told her how lovely she was, how desirable, how deliciously sweet, his half sentences riding on fevered gasps of air.
She needed more.

"Love me," she whispered almost inaudibly.

Eagerly he obeyed. His body fit perfectly to hers, seeking,
finding, possessing, only to be possessed in turn by the seductive cradle of her thighs. His savoring moan mingled with hers.

Just the sensation of smooth skin pressing against hair-roughened, tightly muscled flesh was incredibly erotic. For a time he lay still, reveling in molten pleasure, taking her mouth in a long, melting kiss. Then, inch by exquisitely slow, rapturous inch, he sank into her soft receptive body.

Time stilled; the power to reason vanished in a fiery haze. Yet some part of Eve was thrillingly aware of the beautiful simplicity of their lovemaking. They shared a passionate kiss that flowed into the sensuous adjustment of bodies, the sweet, thrusting joining, excitement that soared higher and higher and then, the ecstatic explosion of all their senses.

Reality returned in fragments of time measured by her easing heartbeat. Eve clung to him, trembling in the aftermath of unearthly pleasure. The memory of her passionate response still shook her with its savage wonder. Sated, euphoric, she expelled a slow breath and found her lips pressed against the damp column of his neck. Her tongue delighted in his dark masculine taste. Eyes shut, she saw, through her caressing fingertips, the magnificent beauty of his broad shoulders and tapering back.

He stirred, murmuring wordlessly. When he raised his head, she put a finger across his lips. "Please, don't say anything, not yet," she whispered.

Silent, Nate moved from her and gathered her close. He couldn't remember ever feeling such luxurious contentment.

Eve could, but for the moment, she was at peace with herself. The shape of his shoulder still conformed to her head. Curving her fingers into the crisp-soft hair on his chest, she lay savoring the splendor of all they had given and received.

There had been no awkwardness or uncertainty, never a false movement, no need to be clever or manipulative. It was simply that he knew her, just as she knew him.

They had made love.

Or had they? Suddenly her mind was sharp and alert again, teeming with so many thoughts and doubts that they fought for precedence. "We did make love, didn't we?"

Her whispery question touched vulnerable areas Nate didn't know existed. He tipped her face to his. She looked so young and defenseless that it wrung his heart. "Oh yes, we made love.

Eve, I know the difference between having sex and making love
with a woman," he assured her. "One becomes a memory you
cherish, the other you forget as easily as a weekend at the
bea—"

Her lashes swept down.

You tactless bastard, he groaned, mentally kicking himself.
A soft oath escaped him. After the glory of what they'd just
shared, it must be as incomprehensible to her as it was to him
that he still couldn't remember her. Frustrated, he half roared,
"Dammit, Eve, I don't know why I still can't remember!
Maybe they performed a lobotomy on me. Who the hell knows
what they do to a man when he's unconscious!"

Her laugh was the sweetest relief. With a whoosh of breath,
Nate buried his hot face in the cool, fragrant mass of her hair.
Feeling nervous and anxious with a woman afterward was a
confusing new experience. This was such a different "afterward." How was he to act with her? Naturally, of course, but
right now he didn't even know what *that* was.

"You're wonderful!" he said a little crazily. "And beautiful—so beautiful you take my breath away."

She broke free and sat up, his extravagant praise twisting her
lips. They were swollen, kissed to the color of a tea rose. Sitting up beside her, he took them with reflaming hunger.

Eve moaned. She couldn't get enough of him, his kisses, his
caresses. Skillful hands branded her skin with the imprint of
each long finger, gliding up and down her back with an exper-
tise that sent quicksilver flashes of heat through every nerve
ending. She loved the incandescent excitement he created. But
she hated knowing that his skillful touch could reduce her to
submission in a matter of minutes.

Her spate of paradoxical emotions swelled into a flood,
drowning her lovely euphoria and, in its wake, leaving her tense
and edgy. Forcing herself to relax, she wove a nail-tip pattern
down his spine to divert his attention from the stiffening taking place in her own. Keep it casual, she warned herself.

Smoothing his mussed hair, she asked, "Tell me, did your
father have a terribly noble brow?"

"A terribly noble brow?" he echoed, nonplussed. His hands
came to rest on her shoulders. "Not that I noticed. Why?"

"Because you do." She had to get away from him—her mood was becoming alarmingly unpredictable. "Noble brows are usually associated with extreme intelligence." She tested his grip. It tightened. "Of course, sometimes they're just inherited, like gray eyes or knobby knees, both of which you also have...." She pondered, then brightened. "How about your grandfather, then?"

Nate burst out laughing, unable to resist the mischief in those violet eyes, the little peaks burning holes in his chest, the seductive bee-stung mouth. "Good grief, woman, you're pure seduction!" he said incredulously.

"Well, I try, Nate," she replied primly, sending him into another mirthful outburst. He looked so lovable, so desirable. With a searing flash of shame, she acknowledged her raw urge to cling to him. *Just like you clung to him that morning, clutching and pleading, all pride and control cast aside in your desperate need to hold him!* The memory could still make her wince, and did. Her sudden urge to lash out at him was so fierce that she had to struggle mightily to contain it. Instead, she slapped his exploring hands. "Now, stop that, I've got to go. Its very late and I'm . . . tired," she ended lamely.

"And regretful?"

"No regrets. I knew what I was doing. Believe it or not, Nate, I'm quite capable of taking this sort of situation in stride."

Nate smiled, but it didn't quite reach his eyes. "What sort of situation is that, Eve?"

"The sort you do very well and I don't, ordinarily. Which is playing fascinating games with fascinating strangers. Not that I have any serious hang-ups about it...." Nate's soft chuckle stung her ears.

"I'm very glad that you don't, ordinarily, and that you have no serious hang-ups," he murmured.

He was watching her with gentle amusement. Eve resented it almost as much as his lordly air of indulgence. Coolly she laughed. "No hang-ups, and no silly little regrets, either. Just for the record, you're the sexiest man I've ever met, Nate. The minute I saw you again, I knew it was inevitable that I'd wind up in your bed."

Nate's mood shifted to match hers. "I knew it was inevitable too, honey," he said, adopting her lazy drawl. "I just didn't know it would take so long." He bent and kissed her rosy lips. "Thank you for putting an end to the sweetest, most maddening frustration I've ever forced myself to endure!"

He cocked his head, looking so sexy that she couldn't resist a needling barb. "Oh, you're most welcome, Nate," she said, carelessly. "Always glad to oblige." Ignoring his quick stir of resentment, she patted his cheek, laughing lightly, hurting somewhere deep inside. "Although I must say the feeling was mutual. It's been a while, but you haven't lost your touch. In fact, if anything, you've gotten better." Her lips formed a sultry curve. "But then, so have I."

Watching the effect her cynical assurance had on him was savagely satisfying. She eased to the edge of the bed.

He stopped her. "I wouldn't know. But damned if I like hearing you talk like that."

No, he wouldn't know. Abashed, Eve swung her feet to the floor. "Me, either. So I'll just shut up and go home. That is, if you'll take your fingers off my shoulders and let me find my clothes?"

Urgently, Nate answered her request with another. "Eve, stay with me tonight. Give me the pleasure of waking up to you in the morning." He grinned, his deliberate arrogance compensating for the uncertainty it concealed. "Which would, of course, give you the pleasure of waking up to *me!*"

Eve stilled. "We've already experienced that particular pleasure," she said, quietly.

Nate said nothing; there was nothing to say.

The silence was almost palpable. She shattered it with a lightly spoken, "Besides, that's something I don't do very well. I'm sure you do—men do seem to have a natural flair for handling the morning after. But it's a bit too intimate for me to take casually. Okay, so maybe I do have a few hang-ups. But they're mine and I happen to like them. So thank you for the invitation, but no thanks."

Even as she spoke, her fingers were entwining the coarse dark curls on his chest with erotic enjoyment. She couldn't keep her hands off him, and he knew it. "I must go," she decided abruptly.

"All right." Nate stood up with her. "But one thing, Eve. What we shared tonight can't be relegated to the usual fun and games. You know that and I know that. So let's dispense with the breezy brush-off routine." Annoyance gave way to indulgence. "I hate to criticize your little act, pretty lady, but it didn't quite come off."

Was she really that transparent? Eve wondered. Feeling foolish, she brushed past him, saying brightly, "Well, then, I'll just have to polish up my little act, won't I!"

"Why? I happen to like you just the way you are. Sweet, unpolished—" he grinned "—and naked."

"Huh," she sniffed. "Well, the latter is easily rectified." Sauntering toward the bathroom, she gathered up her hair and let it cascade through her fingers. Then, with a sensuous stretch of arms above her head, Eve created a visual image of her name.

The low groan behind her was immensely gratifying. A glance over her shoulder noted the effect on his big handsome frame. "My goodness, Nate," she said, looking awed. "You certainly are a *virile* man." Then she beat a hasty retreat into the bathroom.

Nate laughed, too, but his heart wasn't in it. Moodily he turned his attention to dressing. Not that he didn't have cause to feel nervous, he conceded as he zipped his trousers, but there was more to his frustration than being left wanting. Something still nagged at him. Maybe it was Eve's capricious moods, one minute sweet and tender, the way she ought to be, the next secretive and mocking, as if she was putting something over on him.

Ridiculous, he chided himself. One of the things he liked best about Eve was her artlessness. Slipping his feet into fur-lined ankle boots, he jerked down a fresh shirt. She'd just felt a little awkward with all this, he told himself. After tonight, their relationship was bound to improve. At least it had better.

Startled by the trace of grimness infiltrating his musings, he glanced up with an audible catch of breath as she strolled out of the bathroom dressed only in a lace-trimmed camisole and tap pants.

She stopped short as their gazes clashed. The emotionally charged air seemed to crackle with the tension that sprang up between them. What the hell now? he wondered.

"I left my dress out here," she explained. Stepping into the garment, she pulled its floaty skirt over her hips and turned her back for a zip. "You didn't have to get dressed. I have my car."

Impassively, Nate swept aside her hair, and zipped. "I'll see you home. One of my rules is always see a lady to her door."

"Suit yourself."

"I usually do."

"I don't doubt that." She turned, and for a moment they eyed each other like two animals meeting on contested territory.

The tension was too much for Eve. Seeking neutral ground, she walked to the den and put on her coat. "Are you going to the office tomorrow?"

"Yes." Nate donned his leather jacket. "This piracy mess," he explained. "Unpleasant, but..." He shrugged. "I'll be back tomorrow. You will still be here?"

"Yes, of course I'll be here," she said, wondering at his need to check each time he left. Another swift mood shift prompted a provocative comment. "Even though I did get a call from Brian earlier today wanting to know if I could cut my vacation short. Seems I'm being missed around there."

"Brian," Nate repeated, tasting the name. "Isn't he the 'good relationship' you mentioned?"

"Yes. He's also my boss, and getting a little impatient with my absence." She put a hand on the doorknob. Nate's covered it.

"Eve, let's get one thing straight right now. No more games and no more needling remarks about the past. It's over and done with, and as far as I'm concerned, what we did or did not do years ago is totally irrelevant to what we do now. I don't want a one-night stand or a brief affair. I'm interested in a relationship. I assumed you were, too."

Eve struggled with her prickly self and lost. "Maybe you assume too much, Nate."

His eyes narrowed. "Maybe I do. If all you want is a fun-filled fling, then, baby, I'll be more than happy to accommodate you. But if you want something more, then we might as well lay the ground rules right now. After I discern just what it is you want from me, that is," he said with a tinge of sarcasm. "*Do* you want a relationship?"

"Well, I'm certainly not interested in a fling." She tilted her head consideringly. "Just what are those ground rules?"

"Exclusivity, for starters," he said flatly, his masculinity sharply responsive to the challenge glittering in her eyes. "To me a commitment is a commitment all the way down the line. So if you have any idea of seeing another man while you're involved with me, you can just forget it. For as long as this relationship lasts, I expect and demand absolute fidelity, from both of us."

Her eyes shuttered. "For as long as it lasts," she repeated thoughtfully. "You have time limits on your relationships, do you, Nate?"

"No, of course I don't have time limits," he growled. "What I'm saying is that I won't share you." His fingers speared through her hair. "So be forewarned, lovely Eve," he said very softly. "I could be a very jealous lover."

"So can I, and you'd be well-advised to keep that in mind, Nathaniel Wright," came her tart rejoinder. "And if I seem a little too cautious about all this, it's because I haven't had all that much experience with lovers and relationships. I suppose that surprises you, especially since I tried to foster just the opposite impression. But you're so damn *sure* of yourself, Nate. I get a little wild when confronted with such smug male complacence," she accused, scowling her relief as he began laughing.

"Ah, honey, how can I help it?" Nate protested. "Women just keep throwing themselves at my feet!" Delightedly he kissed her pursed lips, as relieved at the easing of tension as she. Laying his cheek against hers, he murmured, "Baby, I'm sorry for—for whatever it was we were fighting about. What was it, anyway?"

"I don't know," Eve confessed with a sigh. Briefly she wondered if Amanda's arrival might not explain some of her feelings. Some, perhaps, but not all. Once she had pleaded with him for a relationship. "Maybe I just liked it too much—being with you, I mean. So now I feel combative." She kissed his firm jaw. "Will you be back early tomorrow?"

His hands slipped under her coat. "As early as possible."

"Good," she replied a trifle unsteadily. "Because I have a surprise for you."

Seven

————

Mary Jo and Patrick were standing on the porch when Eve came in. She was delighted to see them; after tonight she could use some of Patrick's irreverent wit.

She greeted him by inquiring about his health.

Patrick confided that he was feeling feverish and feared he'd caught a cold, or perhaps just fallen in love with Mary Jo, and all things considered, he'd rather have the cold. Then he went whistling down the steps to his car.

"Patrick's always good for a laugh. I don't think he takes anything seriously," Eve said, following her cousin inside. Mary Jo wore her pink artist's smock and a sour expression. "Ah, Mary Josephine, what's got you looking so put out?" she chided. "Patrick's leaving?"

"Patrick's arriving," Mary Jo snapped. "I told him I didn't want to see him tonight, and in no uncertain terms, too. But there he is, giving me that loathsomely boyish smile that can unlock doors all by itself! 'I intend to spend the evening in my studio, working, Patrick,' I said. 'I'd love to watch you work,' he says, and marches right in. You know I don't let just anyone into my studio, Eve. But he did help me lay that new rug in the study off my bedroom—'' She stopped, her cheeks reddening. ''Well, when he finally does decide to make a pass, he's a flaming expert at it, I'll give the man that.''

''Did you respond?''

''Well, yes. I'm not a Popsicle, Eve. Now lay off, okay? Or would you rather stand here wasting breath on Patrick instead of hearing my terrific news?''

''Your terrific news, of course,'' said Eve wisely.

''All right,'' Mary Jo said, grudgingly mollified. ''I'm flying to New York tomorrow morning to 'meet with a gallery owner who's so impressed with my paintings that he's considering a one-man show.' One-woman show,'' she amended.

''Why, Mary Jo, that's super! When did this happen?''

''I got the call this evening. Oh Eve, it's like a dream come true! If it doesn't fall through and if it's even marginally successful, I'll have my year in Paris! Think of it—studying, painting, practically camping out in the Louvre, Versailles, Orangerie!'' Mary Jo gulped air. ''I can't wait! In a fairy-tale dream I'd stay at the Ritz, of course—the museums are all right there around it. But where I stay doesn't matter. Neither does this show, not really. One way or another, I'll have my year in Paris even if I have to swim there and pitch a pup tent under a chestnut tree.'' Her eyes were suddenly too bright. ''Nothing—and no one—is going to stop me.''

''Oh, Mary Jo,'' Eve said softly.

''Now stop it, Eve. I like Patrick—a lot, in fact. But this is much more important to me than any man.''

''Does he know that?''

''Not yet.'' Mary Jo jumped to her feet, exclaiming, ''Gracious, look how late it is—and me having to look halfway intelligent tomorrow! 'Night, honey.'' Leaving Eve with a mouthful of questions, she ran upstairs.

Eve was just completing the aerobic workout that started her vacation days when Mary Jo came downstairs the next morning looking trim and smart in a winter-white suit with navy accessories.

"My goodness, Eve, aerobics this early? Is anything wrong?"

"Just couldn't sleep." After a long deep-breathing stretch, Eve turned to meet troubled dark eyes. "I'm bringing Amanda and Hannah here today."

Apparently her explanation sufficed; Mary Jo nodded sagely. After a few more minutes of varied discussion, she left for the airport.

"Godspeed, honey," Eve called softly to the departing car.

Around ten, she got into her own car and headed for Concord. A tangle of discomfiting thoughts accompanied her on the drive. Last night's unsettling rapture had priority. Although just why it was so unsettling confused her; she had certainly known how Nate's lovemaking could affect a woman. What he had felt was still largely shadowed, but she knew her own feelings had been deeply stirred.

More than just stirred, she amended, recalling the tornadic profusion of emotions. In the privacy of her bedroom, their aftermath had acted as a mirror that reflected a disturbing new image. She had thought she knew herself and discovered she did not. She had felt certain she bore no resentment toward him and found she was wrong. She was not a vengeful person, yet, a time or two she had itched to retaliate for the pain he'd once caused her.

Her intellect knew that pain had not been willfully inflicted. Why, then, couldn't her brain communicate that message to her heart?

Oh, the devil with it, she thought irritably. Let it sort itself out. There were other things to think about. Like reliving the sensation of Nate's big warm hands moving over her body....

Miraculously, she had reached her home without incident. With splendid timing, she crossed the front porch just as the door was flung open on a glad cry of "Mommy!"

Then she was scooping up a wriggly little body, kissing a downy cheek and neck and anything else that presented itself to her greedy mouth. Setting Amanda down, she knelt and looked at her heart's treasure. Soft gold curls as pale as moon dust framed a tiny valentine of a face. Mouse-brown lashes tipped with the same silvery hue fringed big violet blue eyes.

"Oh love, just look how you've grown. Hannah, she's grown so *much*!" Eve accused her housekeeper tearfully. Rolling her eyes heavenward, Hannah agreed that she had.

It was afternoon when they arrived back at the beach cottage. Amanda had napped most of the way and was ready for action. "Let's you and I go for a walk on the beach and let Hannah get a little nap, too," Eve suggested.

Amanda was agreeable. Dressed in jeans and hooded sweatshirts, they raced down a long stretch of beach populated only by birds and a misplaced April wind.

Nate found them there. Watching him stride toward them, Eve felt the bottom drop out of her stomach. Irritably she derided her anxiety. He could not possibly just *look* at Amanda and immediately claim his daughter. There was no obvious resemblance; Amanda was simply, uniquely herself.

Swiftly Eve scooped her little girl up as Nate stopped before them. "Well!" he said. "What have we here? My surprise, by any chance?"

Eve swallowed hard, and replied gaily, "We have here Miss Amanda Sheridan, and yes, she's the surprise." Miss Sheridan promptly suffered a burst of shyness and buried her face in her mother's shoulder.

Nate, chuckling, peeked around the back of Eve's head. "Hello, Amanda! What a lovely little thing, Eve. She's like a fairy princess! Wherever did you find her?" he inquired, smiling at the bouquet of curls tied with pink ribbons. That was all he had to smile at; Amanda firmly refused to unbury her face.

"Oh, I found her one morning sleeping in a red rose growing by the back porch, and I just brought her inside," Eve replied with utter seriousness.

At this absurdity, Amanda giggled and raised her face. "Oh Mommy, I'm too big to sleep in a rose!"

Eve smiled wryly. "Nate, my daughter Amanda. Amanda, this very nice man is my friend, Nate Wright."

"Hello, Amanda," Nate said. "I'm delighted to meet you. Will you come to me?"

Amanda fiddled with her mother's collar as she studied this tall stranger. Her head tipped to one side, and she peeked at him through her lashes. In each cheek a deep dimple flickered on and off. Then, her decision made, she simply held out her arms.

Something shredded Eve's heart as Nate took his daughter. He straightened, holding the child in a firm sure clasp high against his shoulder. Judging her weight with a gentle heft of arms, he nodded judiciously. "I have to agree with you, Amanda, you're certainly much too big to be sleeping in roses!"

Two beautiful faces turned to Eve, violet eyes scowling and gray ones dancing.

The rightness of this moment painfully twisted her heart, but she attributed this to maternal possessiveness. She drew up Amanda's hood and tied it under her pointed chin. "I'm a bit surprised that she'd go to you right off," she told Nate. "She's usually quite shy around strangers, and especially men."

Nate grinned smugly and dismissed any cause for surprise. Females usually found him irresistible. Why should this one be any different?

Wrinkling her nose with a disdainful sniff, Eve reclaimed Amanda and set her free to race the wind.

"Shall we?" Nate asked exuberantly.

"Let's!" Eve agreed. Catching his hand, they raced after the gleeful little girl.

In a stunningly swift about-face, the cold Atlantic floated in a bank of fog, hurling them into an oblivion of blue sky and white ground-level clouds. Then the sky disappeared. Awed by this world of shadows and mist, where even voices seemed hushed and unreal, the two adults walked with the child held firmly between them by the clasp of hands.

Even the silence is white, Eve thought uneasily. She was acutely aware of the strange sense of drifting through a realm where time had no meaning. It enclosed them, surrounded them, pressed softly around them. There was nothing to be seen in front of them or behind them, and her mind drew its own parallel to this elemental illusion. No agonizing past, no uncertain future, just *now*. Just the way they were. How she wanted it to be like that!

But it wasn't.

"Did you get that piracy matter settled?" she asked.

Amanda, tiring of their long walk, stopped and dug her toes into the sand commandingly. Without slowing down, Nate swung the child onto his shoulders. "We've filed charges, yes. So I suppose justice will take its due course...in its undue time. Would you two ladies like to dine with me tonight?" he asked in a lighter tone.

Eve was watching his hands, for sometimes the hands revealed what a man's face did not. She felt ambivalent about the gentleness they displayed with her child, as if she *wanted* to find fault....

"Thank you, but I think not," she answered stiffly. "Amanda's had a full day and is already getting a bit cross. Maybe tomorrow, when she's a little more rested."

"The invitation's still open for you."

"I'd better stay in tonight. I'd never leave Amanda alone on her first night in a strange house. I would ask you to share our dinner, but Amanda eats at five-thirty, and that's a little early for adults." She paused. A brisk wind had come up to shred the fog, and shafts of pink sunlight gilded the curls clinging to Amanda's cheeks. So precious, Eve thought. And those untamable twin cowlicks...

A slow breath steadied her voice. "Since my own hours are so unstable, I try to see that she has the security of a fixed routine. In addition to my regular workweek, I teach two night classes—"

"That's a pretty demanding schedule, isn't it?" Nate interrupted. "Why add it to it?"

"Because a few extra bucks a month comes in handy, that's why," she said too sharply. Hoping Nate hadn't noticed, she laughed and wriggled Amanda's tiny sneaker. "You have no idea how quickly children outgrow things! New shoes practically every six weeks, hmm, Amanda? And we're saving up for Disneyland. Tell Nate what you're going to do when you meet Mickey Mouse!"

Excitedly Amanda launched into a subject dear to her heart. Nate gave her respectful attention. Their voices, one so deep and husky, the other a high chiming lilt, interwove to create a poignant symphony of sound. Eve drifted along on its music, her eyes as turbulent as the sea lapping at their feet.

Realizing they had reached the cottage, she gave herself a mental shake and Nate a bright smile. "Say goodbye, Amanda, then run on inside."

"Goodbye . . ." Amanda hesitated. "Do I call him sir, Mama?"

"Why not call me Uncle Nate—with Mama's permission, of course," Nate suggested, carefully releasing his burden.

"I already have an Uncle Brian," Amanda informed him.

They compromised on just plain Nate, though Nate didn't much like it. "Tell you what," he said, tweaking Amanda's nose, "if I were invited to dinner, I'd bring the ice cream!"

Eve sighed as a curly head nodded vigorous agreement. "Five o'clock, Nate. We're having hamburgers."

"I love hamburgers," he assured. "The kind I fix, that is. Just have the grill hot and leave the rest to me."

"Yes, master," she responded tartly. "Now if you'll excuse me, it's time for cartoons."

He grinned, liking that "master" bit. "I don't suppose I could tempt you with a drink? The sun is over the yardarm, but it's still a good hour before our epicurean feast begins. We could go to that little bar by the marina—scruffy attire a requisite," he said as she glanced down at hers.

"I'd love it. Just let me turn this imp over to Hannah and put on some lipstick first."

A fast five minutes later, Eve reappeared, lipstick on and hair brushed satin smooth. Otherwise, she hadn't bothered with her appearance.

Eyeing the slender figure cloaked in jeans and a cherry-red sweatshirt, Nate fretted, "Maybe we'd better go to the malt shop, instead. That bar doesn't serve drinks to minors."

"No problem. I'll vouch for your age, Nate," Eve told him, then hastily lengthened the distance between her tight-jeaned bottom and his swatting hand. Her heart was light, and laughter floated through her lips. It felt good to know that after all her agonizing, bringing Amanda here hadn't been a mistake, after all. It had gone so well. So far.

"It's going to be a fine day tomorrow," Nate remarked as he started the car. "What shall we do with it?"

Disconcerted by his question, Eve leaned her head back on the plush seat while she considered it. That tomorrow was theirs to do with at all seemed as illusionary as the tissue scraps of fog still clinging to the trees. "You decide. One thing, though. It has to include Amanda."

"Of course it'll include Amanda. You really want me to decide?" Nate asked, sounding pleased. Her nod widened his smile. "I'll put my mind to it, then. Doubtless come up with something grand," he declared so loftily that she poked his ribs. "She's a pretty little thing, that Amanda. And very bright, I think." A devilish grin lighted his sidelong glance. "After all, she liked me!"

"A common female failing, I admit," Eve replied. "But do keep in mind that she's only a baby and thus incapable of sound judgment." His response was a lusty roar of laughter. She clenched her hands against the tentacles of emotion tightening her chest.

Their arrival at the marina coincided with that of a sleek white yacht moving into its slip beside several others resting like giant birds on their way south. Eve was fascinated by this glamorous symbol of wealth and curious to see what sort of creatures inhabited its shining teak decks.

"Have you ever been on a yacht?" she asked Nate. Of course he had. She wondered when. *Perhaps during one of those weeks I spent beside Amanda's hospital bed.* Her hand slipped from his.

She stared unabashedly as three striking women sauntered down the gangplank. They were all clad in boating attire, and each possessed the carefully tousled chic that money does so well. One of them, a petite brunette with slanting gold eyes, squealed Nate's name and flung herself into his arms.

Nate was at least ten inches taller than his beguiling missile. But that didn't hinder Cat Eyes. She simply climbed him.

"Oh, good Lord!" he groaned, laughing as his impetuous friend began splashing impetuous kisses all over his face. The heat of Eve's gaze must have made itself felt. Gently he grasped the tiniest waist imaginable and removed his clinging vine. "Ah...Eve, this is a friend of mine," he said with a hearty chuckle.

"So I assumed," Eve said, and watched his chuckle evolve into a lopsided grin as he raked at his adorably mussed hair.

Apparently too flustered for proper introductions, he plowed on, "Yes, well. This is Eve, and Eve, this is Honi."

"I don't doubt it for a minute," Eve said pleasantly. "Hello, Honi. That's a gorgeous yacht. Is it yours?"

"Daddy's," Honi replied with a limpid smile for Nate.

Eve smiled at him, too, sort of. Under other circumstances, she might have liked the vivacious woman. However, right now she did not, and if Nate had any notion of inviting Honi to join them, he had better think twice.

Nate had too much sense for that. "Well, if you'll excuse us," he said.

"You're excused . . . for now," Honi granted with a ravishing smile. "But if you're not doing anything tonight . . . ?"

"Afraid I am," he said, charmingly rueful.

"Well, perhaps at a later date, then. I'm going to be in town for a few more days, so give me a call if you've got some free time, and we'll share a bottle of bubbly. Could be," she added thoughtfully, "a little friendly conversation might prove enjoyable as well as mutually beneficial."

If Nate noticed Eve's curl of lip, he showed no sign of it. "I'll keep that in mind. Well! Shall we get that drink, Eve? Ladies . . ." Tipping an imaginary hat, he took Eve's arm.

She smiled at him, sizzling mad. "Nate, you're not locked into anything tonight. If you prefer to go off with that tiny sip of bee nectar, why, you just run right along."

She spoke so sweetly that he could have sworn he'd just been frostbitten. Glancing at the possessive hand attached to his sleeve, he grinned to himself. "Now, Eve, do I look like the kind of man who would break one date just because something better came along?" What she muttered rounded his eyes. "Why Elizabeth Eve, shame on you! You know I was only teasing. Besides, I much prefer long-legged blondes to tiny sips of bee nectar," he assured her.

For a moment, Eve carried her cargo of simmering emotions with stony dignity. But she was coping with something far more volatile than anger. Jealousy. The dark primal emotion glittered in her eyes and clenched her hands. What was Honi to him? And what was Eve? Just another long-legged blonde?

She gave him a sideways look that nearly singed her lashes. God, he was attractive! A lock of sun-streaked sable hair had fallen over his brow, giving him that boyish look so irresistible to feminine hearts. The sudden surge of emotion in her own heart attested to that.

"Don't you touch me!" she snapped, overcome with outrage.

His eyebrows shot up.

Glancing at the hand that hadn't made a move toward her, Eve blinked her consternation. "I don't want a drink!" she explained furiously.

One look at her face, and Nate was convinced he didn't want one, either. He was too well-known in this area to tolerate a scene. But damn, she was delicious! He chuckled, then hurriedly backed up a step as absolutely blazing violet eyes smeared sunburn over frostbite. "Now, Eve—"

"Don't you 'now Eve' me! After all that garbage you fed me last night—" Enraged anew, she spun around and headed back to the car.

"Eve, this has gone far enough," he began, opening the door. "Honi is—"

"I do not care to hear what Honi is. I do not care to hear about any of your women, not now, not ever," Eve stated icily. "Is that clear?"

"Lord!" Hastily Nate slid in beside her. "Now dammit, I said this has gone far enough!"

"It has indeed," she agreed. "So why don't you just shut up and take me home and then find yourself another place to eat tonight. I don't cook hamburgers for unprincipled rats."

"I resent being called a rat, Eve, unprincipled or otherwise," he reproved.

"I do not give a damn what you resent," she said through gritted teeth.

His mouth twitched again. Hazily Eve realized that he was enjoying this and that *she* was enjoying this. Justifying either response was beyond her.

"You're nothing but a tomcat. And if you're thinking of kissing me, you'd better think twice, because so help me I'll bite right through your lower lip," she warned dangerously.

"That's a risk definitely worth taking," he decided, and took it with deep male pleasure.

Eve's mind raged on, but her body mutinied. Traitorous teeth refused to bite the mouth that worked such sweet magic. They unclenched and gave him access to everything and anything. He tumbled her onto his lap, and her bones melted. There was no other way to describe it, they simply *melted*.

"I hate you," she said, wishing her voice wasn't so muffled. But her face was embedded in his chest now, and every breath she drew was an aphrodisiac. "I hate the way you smell, too."

"No you don't. Now stop that. Don't try to get away from me," he ordered. "Now what's all this about?" He reared back, remembering. "And what garbage did I feed you last night?"

Her head jerked up. "Commitment and fidelity, that's what garbage!"

"Ah, but only one of us made a commitment," Nate countered softly. "You didn't care to commit yourself, remember?"

Eve stared at him in comical disbelief. "But I thought— Didn't you just take that for granted?" she blurted.

"I never take anything for granted where you're concerned." His voice shaded to irony. "And you didn't exactly jump at my offer, you know. I didn't know if you wanted it or not." He grinned lopsidedly. "Hell, I didn't even know if you wanted *me!*"

It hadn't occurred to her that such a man would harbor the slightest doubt as to the answer he wanted from a woman. "And that's why you were tormenting me with that—that perambulating honeycomb?"

"Turnabout is fair play, isn't it? You've certainly had me walking on coals often enough—and sleeping on them, too...." An eyebrow slanted at her smothered giggle. "I hope this will cease as of tonight? I haven't been getting enough to keep a frog healthy. Sleep, I mean. Among other things." He sobered. "Eve, Honi is strictly business. She's also a mischief maker," he conceded, "but the basis of our acquaintance is the chain of computer marts she and her brother own. Naturally I'd like them to carry my line of software, but as yet we've been unable to come to terms. That's it. So. Yes or no, Eve?"

"Yes. On one condition." She splatted a hand against his chest. "If you ever let another woman plaster herself all over you and mop your face with kisses, I will listen to whatever explanation you can come up with—and then I will kill you."

"Fair enough." Bemusedly he looked around. "I suppose we ought to get you off my lap and us out of this parking lot."

"I suppose." Eve sighed. But she made no effort to remove herself from the cushioning hardness of his lap. Although well aware of her enjoyment, her mind was temporarily absorbed in the puzzling intensity of the emotions she'd just experienced. In order to feel, one had to care. And if the degree of feeling equaled the degree of caring . . .

Oh, nonsense! she snapped at her fluttery fears. Jealousy was merely an undisciplined reaction to the security she'd never had. A second later she caught his mouth in a wild tempestuous kiss that branded him as hers.

The harsh blare of a car horn shattered the blazing spell. Two teenagers in a zebra-striped dune buggy gave them a thumbs-up gesture and some high-spirited, if salacious, advice. Eve's embarrassed gasp provoked a muttered oath from Nate.

He shuddered once and buried his face in her hair with a deeply drawn breath. "You make me ache, you know," he said quietly.

"Oh, Nate, I'm sorry," she said, distressed.

"Me, too—that we're here in this parking lot instead of my bed," he growled.

On the way home, laughing and chattering, Eve mentally replayed the scene at the pier. But there was a dark side to her humorous recall. It had made her realize how very much she still distrusted Nathaniel Wright.

Eight

Shortly after five, Nate returned to the cottage with a sack of groceries under one arm and an ungovernable smile on his face. For a man who was going to sleep alone that night, he felt extraordinarily good. But the screen door was open, and through it drifted a stirringly lovely sound—Eve's lilting voice singing to her laughing daughter.

> "Aman-da, love of my life,
> don't give your poor mother such struggle and strife!
> If you don't put on some shoes this very minute,
> Amanda my sweet, I will paddle your fanny!"

A burst of childish giggles followed. "Oh Mommy, that doesn't rhyme!" Amanda charged, squealing as Eve chased her around the couch.

"It certainly doesn't," Nate seconded, stepping inside.

His smile wavered almost imperceptibly as, for an instant, the two females stared at him as if he were an intruder barging into their world. Then Amanda, still barefoot, ran to him and held up her arms.

So tiny, he thought, picking her up with his free arm and a strange twist of heart. Eve, clad in a shimmery wrap blouse and harem pants, drifted across the room like a windblown leaf. His smile stabilized. "You," he informed her, "are gorgeous."

She waved peach-tipped fingers. "So are you. You're also late."

"The supermarket. It takes time," he replied distractedly. Gauging the heft of his diverse burdens, he reflected, "You know, I think this bag is heavier than she is? I feel like I'm holding a wee bird. Are all little girls so tiny?"

Eve collected her daughter and sent her off to find her fuzzy-bear house shoes before replying. "Amanda's always been small for her age. She barely weighed six pounds when she was born. She's also rather babyish at times, but that's because she's been sick a lot," she added, leading him to the kitchen.

Hannah, busy at the sink, looked up with rounding eyes as his impressive frame filled the doorway. Diffidently, Eve introduced them. He greeted the older woman with beautiful formality, then promptly took command of her domain.

Nate's idea of a proper hamburger was coarsely ground filet mignon shaped into patties and grilled with olive oil and whispers of garlic and fresh basil, then slithered between rounds of crusty rolls, topped by thick slices of beefsteak tomatoes.

"Fantastic!" Eve informed him as she bit into something outrageously delicious.

"Of course it is," he said smugly. "I'm a fantastic cook."

"I hate having to agree with that," Eve muttered just loud enough to be heard.

Despite the opulence of their feast, dinner was not altogether a success. Amanda's fatigue soon degenerated into petulance. Feeling the tension of her own emotional strain, Eve stood up and said to Hannah, "I think this wee bird's had about all the fun she can take for one day. Would you get her washed up and into pajamas, please? I'll come tuck you in in just a few minutes, love," she soothed the drowsy-eyed child.

"Good night, Amanda, and thank you for letting me share your dinner," Nate said, and received a baleful look for his courtesy.

"Amanda, say good-night to the nice man," Hannah prompted.

But Amanda was past the point of being sociable. Firmly she buried her face in Hannah's shoulder. "Don't want to. Go away, man," she ordered crossly.

As the two disappeared from the kitchen, Eve lifted one shoulder apologetically. "Sorry about that, but when Amanda's had enough, she's had enough."

He chuckled. "And like her mother, she doesn't mince words." Twinkling gray eyes looked into hers. "Do you want the man to go away, too?"

"As a matter of fact . . ." She sighed and rubbed her neck. "Nate, I dislike being discourteous, but it has been a long day."

"Of course," he said instantly. "It's been a long day for me, too. A nice one, though." His voice deepened. "Thank you, Eve, for a truly wonderful dinner."

Relieved at his reaction, she reached up and mussed his hair. "Don't thank me. You fixed it."

"But you made it wonderful."

He held out his hand, and Eve took it. Chatting lightly, she walked him to the shadowed deck. The night had turned brilliantly clear and chilly. Nate still held her hand, but otherwise, he made no attempt to touch her. Shivering suddenly, she edged closer.

"In case you haven't realized it yet, tonight was a little special," she offered like a gift. "Exposing Amanda to strangers, particularly male strangers, is very much of the exception rather than the rule. She doesn't meet many of my men friends."

"I'm very glad to be the exception." Bemusedly, Nate tipped his face to the moon. "Beautiful, isn't it?" he murmured, watching its luminous progress.

"Beautiful," Eve agreed, but she was watching him. Raw honesty forced her to acknowledge how desperately much she wanted him. She shuddered.

Thinking she was cold, Nate wrapped her in his warm embrace and kissed her thoroughly before saying good-night. Reluctantly she untangled her fingers from his hair and placed them on his shoulders. "What do you have planned for tomorrow?" she asked breathlessly.

"I don't know yet, but I'll call you as soon as I find out." His hands dropped to her waist. "Well, good night, Eve." He sighed morosely. "You can trust that I'll be doing some tossing and turning tonight...." He looked at her with an odd smile. "You might try doing some of that, too."

"Doing what?" she asked, momentarily confused.

"Trusting me."

Casually she pulled away. "Well, you can't have everything, you know," she said lightly.

"Oh yes I can," came Nate's firm rejoinder. Before she could challenge his words, he branded her lips with a short hard kiss, then strode down the steps.

"Coward!" she cried after him, and heard his soft laughter sweeten the night.

"Strategic retreat," he called back. "Tomorrow, babe!"

"Tomorrow." The word still tastes strange, she thought, opening the door. In the living room, Hannah was waiting. She was short and chunky, with an endearingly homely face and the expression of a bright-eyed squirrel. A snowy apron covered her flowered housedress. Wiping her hands on it, she regarded Eve over the top of tiny gold-rimmed glasses.

"That's a good-looking man you've found," she declared. "Knows how to treat a woman, sure as shootin'. Good with kids, too," she added thoughtfully. "Might not be a bad idea to try catching this one."

"You think he's a keeper, hmm?" Eve murmured, using her father's word for a landed fish big enough to fry. She laughed and hugged the older woman. "Well, seeing as how your judgment is infallible, I'll give it some serious thought, Hannah," she promised solemnly.

The following dawn was ample compensation for Eve's early rising habits. She drank her coffee on the deck, gazing at the splendor of peach-and-gold mist that topped the sea like tinted whipped cream.

In this quiet time, she could think clearly enough to realize that nothing was clear anymore.

Viewed in the light of that conclusion, her persistent skepticism of Nate's words and deeds appeared as more of an asset than a stumbling block. Seeing him with her heart instead of her brain would be very easy, and very foolish. There was too much at stake here to play the fool again, she told herself, without defining what or why.

The sunlight grew stronger, and soon she heard stirrings inside the house. Amanda's fluting voice counterpointed Hannah's soft responses. Her heart lifting, Eve went inside the big, warm, bacon-scented kitchen. So safe and cozy, she thought. Like a fragile bubble.

After a breakfast of toast and coffee she started her exercise routine, but Amanda insisted upon being dressed by her mother. Eve garbed her in jeans, sweater and one bright red sneaker. The other one was nowhere to be found.

"Look under the couch," Hannah called from the kitchen.

"I am looking under the couch—ouch! Amanda, get off my back, please?" Eve requested, laughing. "I'm not a horse, you know!"

"May I join in, or is this a private party?" Nate's deep voice flowed into their giggling fun.

"Oh! Nate, my goodness, what are you doing here? I'm not even dressed yet," Eve said, sitting up.

"So I see," he murmured.

Absurdly, she blushed and tugged at the neckline of her brief red leotard. Flesh-colored tights enhanced her long legs, a fact Nate noted intensely as she stood up beside him. Imprisoning his hands in his pockets, he announced that he'd located a small local carnival and was looking for someone to share the fun.

Amanda tugged at his trouser leg. "I will, I'll go! I am sorry for last night, Mommy says," she said anxiously.

He bowed. "Apology accepted." His smoky gaze danced over to Eve. "I'm ready when you are," he told her.

To her chagrin, Eve felt another rosy blush stain her cheeks. "Amanda, go look in the sun room for your sneaker. It's got to be around somewhere...." She watched her daughter leave the room then spared a glance for the tall handsome man who had invaded her safe morning. "Hannah let you in?"

"Um-hum." His gaze drifted down her. "Those things should be declared illegal," he drawled. "They're far too sexy to be functional."

"They're functional, all right. I have several men in my night class—"

"And they actually watch what your feet are doing? Incredible!"

Her eyes crinkled. "My, aren't you in a good mood!"

"Fan-tastic," he agreed, looking her up and down again.

Amanda was back with the lost sneaker. "I'm going to ride the Ferris wheel!" she informed them.

"Not with me, you're not," said Eve. "I hate the things."

"I happen to love the things, myself," Nate said. "One Ferris wheel ride, coming up, Amanda!"

"Twenty," Amanda said, which was as high as she could count. "And cotton candy and popcorn and candy apples—"

"*No* cotton candy and *no* candy apples, you know that," Eve cut in. "Nate, would you mind waiting until I finish this workout?"

"Not in the least," Nate murmured. Seating himself, he watched her with great pleasure, for the aerobic dance movements of a shapely woman in leotard and tights was a lovely sight.

Sadly, he could tell that his rapt attention made her uncomfortable. A reluctant gallant, he invited Amanda for a walk while her mother finished.

"Her sweatshirt's in the foyer. Be sure and put the hood on," Eve instructed as Amanda and her father left the room.

Amanda located her bright yellow sweatshirt and brought it to Nate. Violet blue eyes flashed up to his, wide and trusting. "Will you put it on, please?"

"Of course," Nate said through a throat that needed clearing. Once again he found himself captivated and mystified by a female. This small creature who looked at him with Eve's own eyes created soft little knots of tenderness in his hard chest, and he didn't know quite how to handle that. Kneeling, he helped her into the garment, taking special care to draw up the hood securely.

Rambling down the beach, stopping now and then to explore the night-sea's bounty, was a peculiar pleasure to Nate. He was seeing the world through a child's eyes, and the world was an awesome place. Fascinating objects abounded—everything from the glistening luminescence of a jellyfish to the mysterious pink tunnel inside a shell and the tiny crab that peeked up from its lustrous depths.

Listening to Amanda's chatter and gleeful laughter was another peculiar delight. The feel of a small hand creeping into his aroused astonishingly fierce protective urges. He supposed his growing fondness for the child to be a reflection of his affection for her mother. As yet those feelings were not clear-cut. But he was aware of his raw need to be with Eve, in whatever form their intimacy assumed, he realized, not just sexually. Sharing a candlelight dinner with her—or just a glorified hamburger in her kitchen—was as sweet and fulfilling as anything he'd experienced with another woman.

"Can we do this every day while Mommy 'roebics?" Amanda's sweet voice scattered his moody thoughts.

"We can if Mommy doesn't mind."

Nate spoke without much confidence; he already knew how touchy Eve was about her daughter, and he had no idea how she'd feel about it.

Eve didn't like it. Private walks and private jokes? No, she didn't like it at all. But since she didn't know why, she could hardly say so. *Especially with my baby's eyes shining like stars,* she thought wryly.

"We'll see, we'll see!" she protested Amanda's happy chatter. "Now if you two will excuse me, I'll hit the shower."

"I'll help you bathe, Mommy, so you can hurry up."

"Me, too, Mommy," Nate offered. "So you can hurry up."

"I think I can bathe alone, thank you very much, Nate and Amanda," Eve said over the lump mushrooming in her throat.

A short time later they were on the road, beginning what Eve suspected would be a memorable day. Sunshine, not too warm and not too cool, spilled upon them like an extravagant gift from the gods. Fruit markets tantalized with their colorful treasures—pumpkins and melons and the first autumn apples. Nate loved watermelon. They bought one and took it to a yellow-grassed meadow, cracked it upon a rock and simply scooped out handfuls of the juicy sweetmeat.

Afterward, a trip to a nearby stream was in order. Nate's large linen handkerchief served nicely as a towel. "What about that?" he asked, eyeing Amanda's melon-blotched sweater.

Eve sighed loudly. "There's a fresh one in that satchel I brought along. I'll get it." As she hurried to the car, she brushed at a spot or two on her garments. Luckily the warmups she wore were the color of their melon. As always with Nate, she was acutely aware of her appearance and hurriedly reapplied lipstick, then retied the richly hued silk scarf holding back her hair before returning to him.

Nate helped strip off the stained sweater. "What happened here?" he asked, noting the tiny puckered scars on the right side of Amanda's rib cage.

"Staph pneumonia. She's had it several times, and treatment is a surgical procedure—a drainage tube inserted through the rib cage. Makes her good as new again, huh, Mandy!" Smoothing the wind-tangled curls, Eve continued, "And not only that, but each time she goes to the hospital, she awakes to a new stuffed animal. You can't see her bed for furry critters! The last time she went in, for a little cosmetic surgery on this pretty dimple they've made her—" she tickled the pucker of scars "—she woke up to find this absolutely monstrous panda beside her. I could have strangled Brian—and now the darn thing takes up half her bedroom!"

A thin smile stretched Nate's mouth. "Maybe I could do that for you. Unless Amanda is wild about monstrous pandas?" he inquired as Eve eased a clean sweater over the child's head.

Amanda shook her head. "No. It stares at me."

"Why, Amanda, I didn't know you didn't like Pan!" Eve said.

"It's got big bug eyes. It stares at me," the child repeated.

"I certainly wouldn't want anything with big bug eyes staring at me," Nate agreed.

"Okay, so we'll stick it in the closet," Eve said a trifle snappishly. "Shall we get this caravan moving again?"

"Oh! Look, Mommy!" Amanda cried, and took off in hot pursuit of a rabbit.

Laughing, Nate stood up and brushed at his jeans. "She's a doll, Eve. Reminds me of my cousin Cathy when she was this age—even has dimples like hers."

"Mary Jo has dimples, too, just like Amanda's," Eve said. Her voice was too raspy. She coughed. "You haven't mentioned Cathy before. Have you other cousins?"

"Several more," he said, losing interest.

Eve did, too, partly from relief and partly from annoyance at letting what amounted to an idle comment unnerve her. She started as two warm hands suddenly cradled her face.

"Good morning, Elizabeth Eve," he said softly. His smile was tender. "Would it be considered improper if I kissed you?"

Caught in an absurdly sweet storm, she licked her lips. "I—I guess not."

His warm mouth slanted across hers, clung for a quickening instant, then reluctantly gave way to propriety. She was trembling inside. Stepping back, she wondered aloud if they were ever going to get to that carnival.

Eventually they did. While Nate and Amanda squeaked with delight as they enjoyed the Ferris wheel, Eve searched out a rest room. When she returned, Amanda had her nose buried in a pink cloud of cotton candy.

"Amanda! What are you doing? Give me that!" Eve exclaimed. Yanking the sticky stuff from the child's hands, she pitched it in a trash can. "You know better than to eat that junk—"

"Hey, whoa there." Nate broke in. "Don't scold her. I'm the one who bought it."

Eve turned on him. "Yes, and you knew better, too. You plainly heard me say no cotton candy. Where did you get the notion that *you* could overrule *my* orders?" she exploded.

Narrow eyed, he responded evenly, "I didn't mean to overrule anyone's orders. I just thought, well, what's a carnival without cotton candy? I was wrong, although I can't for the life of me figure out why that's such a crime. But I was, and I apologize.''

Staring from his taut face to Amanda's quivering lower lip, Eve felt her anger deflate like a pinpricked balloon. She expelled a whooshing breath as the little girl appealed, ''I'm sorry, Mommy. Don't be mad. I won't do it again.''

''Oh, baby, I'm sorry, too. I shouldn't have yelled at you.'' Gathering Amanda into her arms, she glanced at Nate. ''Or you, either. But too much sugar makes her hyper, so I just avoid it altogether. I do have to raise her as I think best....'' She paused, groping for words, knowing as well as he that her anger had been disproportionate to the offense. ''I'm sorry I made such a fuss. I know carnivals and cotton candy go together. Just not in this case. But we both love popcorn!'' she added with a placating smile.

Relaxing, Nate tweaked Amanda's ponytail. ''Okay, popcorn it is. Then we'll ride the Ferris wheel again.''

His easy tone dissipated Eve's tension. ''You're a glutton for punishment,'' she said, taking his hand.

After his sixth ride on the giant wheel, he suggested they try the kiddie cars. She could ride those all by herself, Amanda informed him. After helping her into a red-and-black polka-dot convertible, he sank down next to Eve on a bench.

''How am I doing?'' he asked, groaning as his bottom came in contact with the hard wood.

''Not bad for a novice,'' she granted.

''Not bad? Hah! I'm terrific and you know it.'' Ignoring her disdainful sniff, he continued reflectively, ''I've often wondered how I'd be with kids. A man does, you know. He wonders if he'll ever have any of his own, and if he did, how he'd react to being a father. It's kind of scary, if you want the truth,'' he admitted. ''But I think I might be good at it.''

His soft reflective voice with its endearing trace of pride assailed her with pangs of longing. For a moment Eve wanted very much to confide in him. To see his face when she told him he *did* have a child was a tempting thought in itself. Annoyed at her weakness, she disciplined her reckless urge with a harsh reminder. There was too much at stake here to take unnecessary chances.

"One day isn't exactly a sound basis for judgment, Nate," she countered mildly. "Having fun with them is the easy part. It's the day-to-day responsibility that decides whether or not you're cut out to be a father."

"Can't argue with that." An edge stole into his voice. "But at least I'd be around when they needed me." He laughed, acting casual again. "That's got to count for something."

"It does. What was your father like?" Eve asked, curious.

He hesitated. Body language spoke first as he turned to face her. "I haven't the faintest idea. My parents died when I was two, and I went to live with his sister."

Her heart contracted. He hadn't mentioned being so young when his parents died. "Oh Nate, I'm sorry." She touched his hand. "How sad for you."

"Nonsense," Nate replied, his quick pride rejecting any hint of pity. "Aunt Julie was the most loving family a boy could ask for. She cajoled and threatened and adored me into quite respectable manhood. Alone, because she never remarried after Uncle Seth died. She was one great lady," he ended very softly.

"You didn't feel bitter about not having a father figure?"

"I wouldn't dare," he said, chuckling. "Aunt Julie didn't hold with self-pity."

"But you still needed one," Eve persisted.

"Sometimes." He shrugged. "Mostly I just accepted the way things were. I remember this friend I had all through grade school. His name was Larry, and he had the kind of father you'd choose if people had such choices. He let me tag along on camping trips, taught me how to catch a fish ... Sometimes, after ball practice, he'd take us to a movie and we'd load up on popcorn and Milky Ways. And sometimes I ached to have a dad like that." He grinned. "Not that he was a soft touch, you understand. Infractions of his rules were dealt with sternly, and if *I* was the infractee, then I got walloped right along with Larry. Then Aunt Julie would call him up and thank him kindly for sparing her the job."

The sudden spate of words surprised Nate. While not exactly the strong silent type, he acknowledged humorously, he wasn't one to go on about himself. Quickly he reversed her question.

"How about your dad?"

She looked away.

He tilted an eyebrow. "Or have you already told me?"

"I have, but . . ." That delicate lift of shoulder expressed acceptance. "He was wonderful. Too easygoing to stand up to Mother, but we usually managed to get around her if I thought I'd perish from the lack of whatever. Even so, I had a strict upbringing. Lots of 'oughts' and 'musts' and 'shoulds' and 'thou-absolutely-shalt-nots!' He's been gone six years, and I still miss him. He was a natural when it came to being a father."

"Which brings up an interesting point," Nate mused, returning Amanda's wave. "Why hasn't she got one? Why *haven't* you married, Eve?" Alert gray eyes fastened on her face. "Could it be that you're still carrying a torch?"

"Not likely," she snorted. "Even the brightest torch goes out after a while."

"But you did love him, once."

"I thought I did. Once." A coldness filtered through her eyes. "But he was a careless man, careless with a woman's heart."

"He was also a fool," Nate said. His voice was steely with the anger that fired him every time he thought of that faceless fool. "Amanda's a beautiful child. Had she been mine . . ."

"Had she been yours?"

"Then she'd *be* mine. Maybe you're lucky he did skip out on you."

"He didn't exactly skip out on me," Eve said without thinking. "He has no idea he has a child."

"But you said—"

"I know what I said. I . . ." Floundering, berating herself for her prideful stupidity, she shot to her feet. "Since I knew he wouldn't want it, I saw no reason to bother him with his little mistake." Gripping the rail, she watched Amanda come into view. The ride was slowing. Eve followed the polka-dot car to a stop.

"Then I'd say you really are lucky," Nate said close to her ear. "Lucky that he doesn't know, and lucky it wasn't me. Because I'd do everything in my power to claim my child, regardless of how her mother felt about me.''

Eve did not reply for several very long seconds. When she did, her voice was remarkably light and airy. "Well, lucky for me that she's not yours, then!''

Stepping in front of him, she reached out and claimed her heart's treasure.

Nine

——

I think this one needs a long soak in a hot tub!'' Mary Jo said, nuzzling the grubby child she held. The two had enjoyed a most satisfying reunion, which included a running monologue of Amanda's fun-filled day.

"She's not the only one." Eve sighed. "Hannah, would you do the honors? Umm.... Is that homemade bread I smell?"

"Sure is," Mary Jo affirmed. "I've already eaten three slices." Releasing Amanda to the housekeeper, she sat down at the kitchen table. "So tell me, how did it go with Nate and Amanda?"

Eve grabbed a plate and joined her. "Better than I had hoped for. He has patience, and Lord knows it takes patience." In between bites of freshly baked bread slathered with creamery butter, she related the more pertinent details of their day.

"Any man who can ride the Ferris wheel that many times is either wacky or sainted," was Mary Jo's opinion. "But why'd you get so uptight about that incident with the cotton candy? I know how you feel about junk food, but an exception now and then isn't going to kill her, Eve."

"I know, I know. But I was just suddenly so *furious*." Eve wiped her fingers one by one. "It wasn't the candy, it was him," she confessed. "I'm the one who decides what's best for Amanda—it's *my* job, *my* right, not his."

"But that will have to change, won't it?" Mary Jo prodded gently. "Unless you've changed your mind about all this?"

"I—" Eve broke off as Nate's quiet declaration shot to mind. *"Lucky it wasn't me. Because I'd do everything in my power to claim my child."* The chill prickling the back of her neck was but a pale echo of her initial reaction. In those excruciatingly long seconds before her airy reply, she had felt a sudden, wild, desperate need to flee him and be quit of this dangerous gamble she was taking.

But even then she'd known it was too late. Her heart's immovable dream had joined forces with passion's irresistible hunger, a force that held her to him like iron to a magnet.

With pained humor, Eve wondered if her mind wasn't muddled enough already without adding to it. But she didn't seem to have a choice. At least there was one area still firmly under her control, she thought defiantly. Nate couldn't claim what he didn't know he had.

Of course, when she did tell him . . . Irritably she shook her head, vexed at her inability to reconcile two opposing urges, wanting to tell him and dreading to tell him. I'll cross that bridge when I come to it, she decided, discarding the crumpled napkin.

Looking up to encounter quizzical brown eyes, she made a face. "No, I haven't changed my mind." She glanced at her watch. "Well, he'll be back here in an hour, so let's get on to you. What happened in New York?"

"Bingo!"

"Bingo?" Eve's puzzlement vanished. "You're having the show? Terrific! When?"

"In three weeks. Not only that, but I'm getting a small grant!" Mary Jo crowed. Her excitement was infectious, and feminine voices mingled in a lyrical volley of questions and answers. "I called Patrick last night and told him all about it. He thinks I'm crazy, of course, running off to Paris when I could be with him." Meeting Eve's observant gaze, she grimaced. "You think I'm crazy?"

Eve squeezed her hand. "Nope. Just another confused-all-to-hell-and-gone woman trying to walk forward while looking backward. Got to expect a few stubbed toes with that tricky feat!"

"Well, I never heard of anybody dying from a stubbed toe yet," Mary Jo returned drolly. Visibly relieved by the injection of humor, she reached under the table and brought up a long striped dress box. "For you," she said rather grandly. "A birthday present."

"But my birthday's still a month away," Eve protested as she opened it.

"So I'm a little early. You like it?"

"Like it? I love it!" Eve breathed, holding up the chic frock. The black knit bodice was simplicity itself: plunging neckline, long thin sleeves and a sliver of a belt. The skirt was made entirely of soft, pale gray silk petals.

"Found it on sale." Mary Jo waved away her thanks. "Let's go upstairs and make you fit the dress. I'll get out my curling iron. We'll try some of this liqueur I bought, while we're at it. Celebrate a little. Its Framboise. Made from fresh raspberries, it says here."

Laughing, Eve accepted the small cordial glass along with her cousin's opinion. Anything made from fresh raspberries couldn't be too dangerous.

An hour or so and three glassfuls later, she stood before the mirror staring at herself with delighted disbelief. The dress was a knockout. Her hair had been caught up in a careless pouf of curls atop her head, and straying tendrils danced around her dainty ears.

"Oh Mommy, you look *pretty!*" Amanda breathed, scampering into the room. "Am I pretty, too?"

"Kiddo, you're a living doll," Mary Jo asserted, picking up the pajama-clad child. "Ah, the doorbell. Tell you what, we'll go let him in, then we'll all go to the kitchen so your mommy can make a splashy entrance," she said, and sped out the door.

Eve faced the mirror again, her expression turning wistful.
The image confronting her was a fraud. She wasn't that confident, sexy, uninhibited creature in the mirror—was she?

Startled by the infusion of doubt, she stared at herself ana-
lytically. Which should she believe? Self-image or mirror image? Mother or woman? Both, of course. But had she fixated
on one at the expense of the other? Her name was quintessen-
tially female. Was *she*?

Nate seemed to think so. Standing at the foot of the stairs in
the foyer, he watched Eve's graceful descent with a smile as
frankly sensual as the desire flaring in his smoky eyes.

Wetting her lips was more an act of anxiety than flirtation.
Her nerves were suddenly strands of spun glass. The tall, ele-
gantly clad man she approached was a formidable challenge.
He demanded so much of her with that air of expectation.
What if she couldn't live up to it? Hating her self-doubt, she
tipped back her head and met his rapt gaze.

"Wow. You're beautiful," he said with a wicked grin. But he
made no attempt to touch her. Realizing why, filled her chest
with a lovely sensation. She guessed he was feeling a little nervous himself.

"Hi, Nate," she replied, and kissed his clean-shaved cheek.
He smelled so good! The lovely feeling expanded until her
spirits soared like an untethered balloon. Although there was
still a tremor in the fingers he kissed a bit awkwardly, she preceded him to the door with a haughty carriage and a provocative sway of hips. Funny how much woman-power there was in
a smashing new dress, she reflected, glancing over her shoulder.

Eve paid no attention to his startled look. Lightning danced
in the sky, and the excitement fermenting in the pit of her
stomach seemed to feed on the charged air. In the car she sat
close to him. She liked the iron feel of him and stroked his thigh
a little before he captured her marauding fingers with a husky
laugh.

He'd made dinner reservations at the posh Harbor Club, a
mahogany-and-rose-colored room with tall mullioned windows. Although enjoying the atmosphere, Eve wasn't hungry,
and she merely toyed with her elaborate salad. Apparently Nate

had lost his appetite, too. He delightedly watched her, baiting her, enjoying her. His gold-flecked eyes twinkled, and his lean cheeks were scored by curving lines of laughter.

She pushed her plate aside. "I'm tired of this place. Let's go somewhere a little less dignified."

"Your wish is my command," Nate said. He signaled for the check. "How about that party I mentioned?"

"Why don't we have our own party?" she suggested. Her smile shimmered in the eyes regarding him through a thicket of lashes. "A private party. At your house."

Nate locked the door and leaned back against it, watching Eve as she sauntered to the couch and tossed her evening bag upon it. The faint trace of primness in her manner was as provocative as a glimpse of black lace beneath a khaki shirt.

She slipped off her pumps. Then, languidly, she peeled off her cashmere wrap, making of it an act so erotic he forgot to breathe.

Hungrily he reached for her. Laughing, she spun away.

"Take down my hair?" she requested.

Before he could comply, she wound her arms around his neck, her eyes half-closed as she looked up at him. With heady pleasure Nate pulled her tightly against him and took her lips in a hotly passionate kiss.

She let him hold it until the heat smoldering in his loins flared into lambent flames. Then she slid out of his arms and repeated her request. Request? More like a royal command, he thought, chuckling as coral-tinted fingernails held him at bay.

Obediently he began extracting pins. There was a delicious new wildness about her that raged in his blood, but Nate wouldn't have altered her coquettish mood for anything. She was letting down her hair tonight in more ways than one, he realized.

When the golden mass spilled into his hands, she stepped away and turned her back to him. "Unzip, please," she ordered. He obeyed. Peeling the dress down her sleekly nyloned legs, she stepped out of it and carried it to his bedroom.

Nate followed. Ignoring him, she snapped on his bedside lamp, laid her frock over his valet chair, shook back her hair.

Nate waited as her naughty amethyst gaze did a slow waltz down his taut frame. She laughed and circled him, moving with the delectable fluidity that captivated him so.

Laughing, he caught her, lifted her high in the air and whirled her around. He felt drunk, even though he'd only had a glass of wine. She was intoxicating, this unfamiliar Eve who peered at him from shining violet eyes. She was indescribably lovely and so sexy he blazed with excitement.

Together they rid him of interfering clothes. At some point he realized she still wore most of hers and hurriedly set to work on this oversight. He took off the strapless bra that barely covered her nipples. The sleek little half-slip drifted to the carpet. Then there was nothing between them. Except panty hose.

"Panty hose!" he muttered indignantly, trying to get a non-destructive grasp on the fragile garment. Impossible. The slippery silk stockings offered no safe hold, and the black lace panty looked as though it would come apart like cobwebs in his clumsy fingers. Whoever invented the things should be shot, in his opinion.

"Oh really, Nate," she sniffed, and took them off herself.

Sensibly, Nate picked her up and carried her to bed.

He lay down beside her, his body hard and tense with arousal. He lowered his head and plunged deeply into the sweetness of her mouth. The tasting was long and luxurious, with all his senses concentrated in it. When he felt her quivery shudder, he drew back to look at her. What he saw gripped his heart.

Colors and textures exploded at him with the strength of powerful emotions. The linens were pale green satin. The pillow beneath her tumbled hair was voluptuously soft and plump. In the peach-hued light, her skin gleamed warmly, the golden moss nested at the junction of her thighs just a translucent shade darker. Her mouth was pink and swollen from his kisses. The sensation of falling into her deep purple eyes was so real he trembled.

The allure of rose-tipped breasts compelled his mouth. With the tip of his tongue, he charted the faint white traceries radiating down her belly like enticing guidelines to hidden treasures.

Moaning, Eve covered his pleasure-giving hands with hers. Her need to take him in was a hammering urgency. But when he moved to cover her body with his, she stopped him. Being in control, she discovered, was a powerful aphrodisiac. It created a strange and exciting mix of emotions. A desire to defy and a desire to submit. One was fully as strong as the other. She slid from beneath him.

Her low laugh taunted his groan. "Now, Nate, play fair," she reproved, leaning over him. "Close your eyes—it's my turn."

Laughter rumbled deep in his chest as Nate obeyed. He heard the rustle of sheets, felt cool fingers pressing him down into their slippery softness. He waited, his breath abated. And then the air left his lungs in an erotic rush of excitement. Eve was exploring him as thoroughly as he had her.

His body felt tight and feverish. Nerves danced and leaped under his skin wherever she touched him. The tips of her nails set fire to rippling musculature. Hot feathery kisses spread the fever across the breadth of his shoulders, up the strong column of his neck and around his firm jawline. A finger probed through his chest hair and located his hard male nipple. Her teeth closed around the tight brown bud while her fingers channeled the flames downward, moving so slowly on his burning skin he thought he'd die from the waiting. She nipped and touched and tantalized until the white heat of rapture filled his mind and body and he could stand no more. Blindly he pulled her down atop him.

With a soft cry of triumph, Eve surrendered to his dominance. Gripping her hips, he filled her, and she took him deeper. Torrents of sensation poured through her. She shut her eyes, and star bursts of pleasure danced behind her lids. She could feel his shuddering breaths. Hers came as rushing little gasps, faster and faster. Flinging back her head, she grabbed his anchoring arms and rode her wild whirlwind to the brink of ecstasy and beyond.

Nate held back, waiting, savoring her pleasure. Then, thrusting his hands into her streaming hair, he brought her mouth to his and plunged into the same exquisite madness.

* * *

Rain lulled them, time drowsed by. Beneath her breasts, Eve felt the beat of his heart, slow and steady again. She thought he was sleeping, but when she stirred, his arms tightened.

Wind whined outside the windows. She shivered. He drew up the sheet and tucked it around her. One big hand moved through her hair in idle caress. She closed her eyes and let herself drift like a leaf on a summer stream.

The caressing hand moved lower, light and sure on her skin. "I don't hear you doing it," he said close to her ear.

"Hear me doing what?"

"Purring," he replied with a whispery chuckle. "You said you purred like a kitten when someone rubbed your neck."

"I did?" Eve murmured, mildly perplexed. She couldn't remember having told him that. But apparently she had. She felt too drugged from love's narcotic afterglow to wonder when. "What a dumb thing to tell you, though I do feel like that," she confessed as his fingers worked their magic. "I also feel a little embarrassed about the way I've acted tonight."

"Why? I loved it. You were wonderful. It was wonderful."

"True." Her lips touched his chest. "What did you love?"

"Everything. The spontaneity, the laughter. The fun."

She lifted her head. "The fun?"

"Yeah, the fun. The way you flirted and led me on. Drove me crazy just trying to anticipate what you were going to do next." Another deep chuckle vibrated against her sensitive breasts. "A gorgeous way to go crazy." His fingers stilled. "Did you ever do that to me before?"

"No." Her lashes fluttered against his throat. Sex and fun. She had never coupled one with the other. Sex was supposed to be taken seriously. "I'm not sure that was me doing it this time, either. Could have been the dress. Or the Framboise."

"It was you."

Eve smiled, skeptically at first, then with pleasure, for it was a pleasing thought and he sounded so positive about it. Yielding to his ravishing warmth, she gave a little purr of approval as his fingers started moving again.

He laughed, a satisfied male sound, and began stroking the lithe, silken muscles running from shoulders to buttocks.

Instantly responsive to the velvety friction, Eve rose up on her palms and lowered her lips to his jaw. The erotic sensation of bristly male flesh against her tongue quickened her pulses. She kissed him, outlined his firm lips, tasted the dusky man-scents that slicked his skin.

She needed him to love her again. Or did she just need him? At the moment, it didn't matter. The two needs were one.

Desire flared, astonishing in its gentle intensity. Slowly, still locked in a bewitching tangle of limbs, he turned on his side and pressed her down into the sheets. They kissed, and the kiss was deep and endless. It blocked the past. It drew them back into the turbulent pool of rapture's heady excitement. His rising passion was a tempestuous singing in her bloodstream. Hers evoked a curiously safe sense of vulnerability. She didn't understand that, but it wasn't important. The man who positioned her beneath his powerful body was her whole world tonight.

Nate sensed the alteration in her. He saw it. There was no wariness on the face he watched so intently, no hint of ice-glazed violets. She held back nothing from him. Even his name had a new sound. It shaped the lazy smile that curled her lips when she whispered it. Gazing into the undefended depths of her eyes wrung his heart in strange and lovely ways.

It seemed to go on for hours, this sweetly unfrenzied joining. They were learning how to please each other, and they had all the time in the world in which to do it.

"Now, Eve?" he asked without urgency.

"Nate, oh Nate.... Love me, please love me," she responded with odd intensity. And very abruptly they were rushing through the same rich, sensual realm of pleasure as the first time.

The world came back slowly, with great quietude. Pillowing her head on his shoulder, Nate turned his face into her hair with an exquisite sense of completeness. Their lovemaking had fulfilled two equally powerful desires. The first time, with its fast furious rhythm, had satisfied sexual hunger. But the other, so intensely sweet and tender, satisfied the soul. He wondered if she felt it too, this closeness, this deep sense of intimacy that soared above physical contact. He felt too vulnerable to ask. It mattered too much.

Absently he caressed her tender nape. There were other questions he wanted to ask, questions about the past. Hers, his, theirs. But she was so defensive about questions, and he didn't want to spoil this sumptuous contentment. Besides, he hated slamming into invisible walls. And she was purring, a breathy sound from deep in her throat.

Her hazy purple eyes opened, warm and receptive. She smiled and he kissed her lips. "Tell me how it was with us, in Vegas," he said with a need to know that overruled common sense.

Eve closed her eyes to shut out his compelling gaze. She felt wondrously at peace with herself and wanted to enjoy it as long as possible. "It was good between us. Very good," she replied, her tone neutral. "Tender, passionate. Not too long lasting—we only had the one night—but still very satisfying."

Nate stopped stroking. "Only one night? But you said we had a weekend."

"We did. But the first night we just . . . became acquainted. Or at least stopped being strangers. We went casino hopping, gambled away your money, had a champagne breakfast on your hotel balcony. Very romantic. First time I'd ever tasted expensive champagne. And certainly the first time I'd tasted a scrambled-egg-and-caviar blini. I thought it was awful. But you seemed to like it. Finished off yours and mine, too," she said over a huge yawn. "Then we talked for a while."

"About what?"

"Little things, mostly." She shifted position just enough to watch his face as she spoke. "For some reason we got on the subject of childhood pets, I remember, and I told you about my talking budgie and you told me about the time you rang a friend's doorbell wearing two huge blacksnakes draped around your neck. Tongues flicking and heads darting—your friend's mother answered the door and fainted dead away!"

"Really? I told you about that?"

"You were eight years old then, and collected anything that walked, slithered or crawled across your path," Eve murmured, her lips curving as a mental image of that rascally little boy flitted across her mind.

"Yeah, I remember. Aunt Julie claimed she was continually on the verge of a nervous breakdown," he said with a boyish laugh. "What else did I tell you?"

"Generalities, for the most part. A few basic background details—that you were divorced, but didn't care to discuss it, that you worked with computers, a boring subject, that you delayed college to knock about the world for a while and loved every minute of it, and what about me?" Irony laced her voice. "At which point I told you everything that happened to me from the day I was born."

"Tell me again."

She made a comical moue. "For heaven's sake, Nate, once is enough!"

His protests were mixed with another rich laugh, and she wanted to oblige him. But a mixed bag of feelings had shredded her blissful state of mind, including one emotion so disturbing that she shrank from acknowledging it as she looked at him. The rugged features now softened by loving, the tug of a cowlick standing at attention, the blue-gray eyes so warm on her face, all worked together to flood her with violent yearning.

She rolled onto her back and pulled the sheet to her chin. "I suppose there've been a lot of women since then," she mused.

"No, not all that many." Nate turned on his side and bent an arm beneath his head. "I'm not comfortable with brief affairs. I prefer deeper involvements. Or would, if I could have worked up the feelings to match," he added ruefully. "But none of them ever came to anything."

"With good reason, I'd say," she replied with a slight twist of lips. His words skittered through her mind, leaving an oily slick of anxiety. Eve was weary of feeling anxious. She sat up, bringing the sheet with her. "I must go."

"Go! Eve," Nate groaned as she swung her feet to the floor and stood up, sheet and all. Grabbing a corner of the puffy coverlet, he followed the supple body draped sarong-style in lustrous green satin to the edge of the bed, there to wrap both arms around her hips and scowl up at her. "It's far too soon to leave, even if I could let you go. Which I can't," he stated, nuzzling her soft belly.

Cool violet eyes flicked him like the tips of a velvet whip. "Can't you? You found it easy enough that morning in Vegas. In fact, as I recall, you walked out without a backward glance."

Taken aback by the bitterness implicit in both tone and words, Nate quickly released her and reached for the navy silk robe he'd tossed over the footboard that morning. Equally quick, she stepped back a few paces. Judging by her expression, she was as startled as he by what she'd said. Her chin snapped up in a gesture he could read like a book. She hadn't meant to say it, but now that she had, she was sticking with it.

While Nate pulled on the knee-length robe, Eve stood haughtily in place, a disinterested observer, ramrod straight and proud, almost elegant in her improvised gown.

My defiant goddess, he thought with a bleak touch of whimsy.

The silence was as awkward as two ex-lovers trapped in an elevator. He sat down again, his mind racing. He had assumed they'd parted on friendly terms. Obviously he'd assumed wrong. But assume was *all* he could do. So how was he to counter her accusation? Even if he had possessed the glib tongue he wished for so devoutly, there were no weapons in his arsenal, no conciliatory facts to deflect the chill of her bright gaze. Just speculation, and a gut instinct that said she was mistaken.

But how to convince *her* of that? He doubted he could. But he had to try, even if it meant exposing an extremely personal failure to a woman whose opinion could cause him considerable pain. He tightened the robe's thin tailored sash until it bit into his waist. "Eve, sit down, please," he requested quietly.

She took the massive white suede chair diagonally across from the bed. Her color-washed cheekbones were taut with self-annoyance. "Nate, let's not get into what I just said, okay? It isn't important—"

"It is important," he rebuked. "I can't believe it would ever be easy to leave you, under any circumstances. Necessary, maybe, but not easy. Look, I've already told you I had just come through a bad divorce when we first met. It was tough

giving up on my marriage and even tougher giving up her.
Fortunately for her, she didn't have that problem. Shortly before we broke up, she'd started back to college and felt she
needed a math tutor. So she hired one. Nice enough guy, I
thought. So did she, apparently. They were married as soon as
the divorce became final."

"You blame her for that?" Eve inquired.

"I did then. I felt so gut-wrenching hurt and bitter, so *hu-
miliated*. . . ." Nate expelled a hard breath. "Eventually I came
to terms with myself, of course." He laughed dryly. "Not much
else I could do. But to answer your question, no, I can't lay all
the blame on her. Love isn't something you can switch on and
off like a faucet. It withers and dies, from a variety of causes,
I guess, but hers died from my simple neglect. Like a flower you
forget to tend. . . ."

The hand he dragged through his hair came to rest on the
back of his neck. "Well, that's all water under the bridge—or
it would be, if it didn't affect you. But it did. Still does, evidently, and I'm sorry about that." His tone leveled. "But it's
very possible I might be even sorrier had I not walked out. You
could have wound up really getting hurt instead of just your
pride scratched. Maybe I had enough sense to know that."

"Maybe." Her mouth quirked. "Maybe I'm the one who
lacked sense, trying to make something out of nothing . . . like
you're doing right now."

"Eve," he sighed. "Was I insensitive, careless? Damn, I hate
not knowing."

"Neither. In fact, you were very nice. A gentleman." The
corners of her lips curved drolly downward. "Which made it
all the worse, of course." Hitching at her sheet, she slipped out
of the chair and picked up her undergarments. "Look, Nate,
I'm embarrassed enough about hanging on to my petty resentment all these years. Don't make it any worse by being even
nicer. I see your point—" She raised a silencing hand. "No, I
really do, and it's all right."

"Is it?" he asked quietly.

She laughed. "I guess it has to be, doesn't it?"

"I guess it does."

The resignation in his low voice caught at Eve's soft heart. Although he'd done little more than reinforce her initial impression of what she had been to him—a masculine escape, she reminded herself bluntly—his concern for her feelings was obvious.

So was the devastating blow his wife's infidelity had dealt his proud soul. Imagining his hurt flooded Eve with sympathy. She ached to hold him, ached to comfort. But doubtless someone else had already done that. Several someones, she thought with just enough cynicism to propel her toward the bathroom rather than into his arms.

Ten

The storm that blew through at dawn left behind clear skies and lower temperatures. Eve awoke to a day as crisp and bright as hardrock candy. Shivering a little, she closed the window. A thin film of mist bedewed the glass. She drew a heart on one pane and pierced it with an arrow that bore Nate's name.

A breath shuddered through her lips as Eve studied her handiwork. She'd drawn exactly what she felt.

A brush of fingertip removed Cupid's invasive arrow. If only it was so easy in real life, she thought. How had she let herself come to care so much? How could she have prevented it?

Eyeing the sleep-tumbled hair and pink-pajama-clad image reflected in her dressing table mirror, she pulled a face. "Oh, Eve, you dear little fool, you," she whispered. "The things you get yourself into!" Her eyelids stung, and she gave them a hard swipe.

Downstairs she could hear Amanda's voice raised in protest. Then a high-pitched squeal preceded the waterfall of giggles spilling up the staircase before Amanda burst into the room and flung herself into her mother's arms.

"Mommy, help me, help me! Hannah's gonna get me!"

Laughing, Eve held her mischievous daughter fiercely tight. "Why is Hannah going to get you, hmm?" she asked as the housekeeper came puffing into the room like a miniature steam engine.

"She won't let me dress her until I find her 'joolry,'" Hannah said, hands on hips. "I told her we didn't bring any—"

"Oh, she's talking about those plastic snap-beads Brian got her. They're in my jewelry case. I'll dress her, Hannah," Eve soothed. Upending the merry child, she dumped her on the bed and flopped down beside her, a growling monster who ate plump little tummies for breakfast.

"Mercy!" Hannah said, and fled the clamorous room.

Eventually Amanda was stuffed into striped overalls and her favorite sweater. With the treasured beads dangling most satisfactorily around neck and wrist, she romped off to the glassed-in sun porch that now doubled as her playroom.

Eve replaced her own pajamas with a sleek white leotard and matching tights. Twisting her hair into a thick braid she coiled it atop her head without regard to appearance. The delectable smell of coffee led her to the kitchen. Cup in hand, she strolled into the cool spacious den that accommodated her aerobic routines.

She was doing push-ups when two shining leather boots planted themselves just inches from her nose. She sat back on her haunches, her throat tightening as her gaze inched up a heart-stopping length of lean black jeans to a red wool shirt. Nate's skin was ruddy from sun and wind, his dark hair wonderfully tousled. The smile glowing in his blue-gray eyes threatened to overwhelm her with visceral longing.

Unbidden, her guard went up, along with a delicately arched eyebrow. "Hi, Nate. You're here awfully early. Any reason?"

He cocked his head. "I thought we'd take Amanda to visit a farm."

"A farm? Oh, I don't think she'd care for that. We live on the outskirts of town, practically in the country." With a lithe twist of muscles, Eve grabbed her towel and came up beside him. He smelled of after-shave and clean cold air, a spine-tingling combination. The vitality he exuded made her feel slightly dizzy and in need of a deep breath. Inhaling, she blotted her damp face. "Anyway, it may be too chilly for outside activities," she added, frowning warningly as Amanda dashed into the room.

"It's gorgeous outside," Nate informed her. He bent down to Amanda. "Would you like to go visit a farm, Amanda? They've got kittens and puppies to play with, ducks to feed—"

"Oh yes! Please, Mommy? I'll be warm, I promise!" Amanda pleaded until her mother gave resigned agreement.

Looking shamelessly pleased with himself, Nate leaned down again and whispered loudly, "Now ask her if we can take another walk while she finishes her workout."

"Can we, Mommy? Please?"

"Please, Mommy?" Nate importuned so comically that the little girl giggled.

Eve stiffened, instantly resistive to the conspiracy of twinkling eyes and identical smiles. Chiding herself, she took another deep breath and threw up her hands with a husky laugh. "Okay, okay! Run find your jacket, Amanda."

Amanda dashed off with a whoop of excitement.

Smiling, Eve looked up at Nate and murmured, "Looks like I was wrong about the farm. What other surprises do you have up your sleeve?"

He slipped his hands around her waist. "That's all for today. Weather permitting, tomorrow is picnicking beside a stream, walking through the woods, stuff like that. Is that suitable?" he checked.

"Yes, she loves stuff like that. Nate, why are you doing this?" At his puzzled look, she added, "Going to all this trouble just to amuse a child, I mean."

"Because I like to, of course. It's entertaining, watching a child's reaction to things you take for granted. Makes everything new and interesting in ways you've long since forgotten," he said reflectively.

Eve gazed into his eyes, wondering involuntarily if his reason was really that innocent. Was he playing the familiar game of making a fuss over the child to get to the woman? Swiftly she rejected the foul thought. His manner was too warm and natural for such deviousness. Besides, he had no need of it, she reminded herself wryly. He had already gotten to the woman.

As an apology of sorts, she cradled his face and pressed her mouth to his in a soft kiss.

"Umm, you taste good," he whispered on her lips. "You taste—" he sampled it again "—like no one else in the world."

Hearing Amanda's approaching footsteps, Eve hastily detached herself from him and cleared her throat. "You're rather unique yourself," she murmured before turning to her daughter. "Well, I see Amanda's found her new bucket. We thought we'd lost it," she told Nate brightly. "You two run along, and I'll join you as soon as I shower and dress."

"Oh goody! You can help us find shells," Amanda said. Taking Nate's hand, she hurried him to the door. "This is my shell bucket. Mary Jo got it for me in New York," she said so importantly that he chuckled to himself.

He paused, wanting to share the moment. But Eve was already running up the stairs, and Amanda was pulling him forward with all her determined strength.

The little girl towed Nate down the steps and across the sand. Her voice rose and fell like scraps of music floating on the wind. Nate listened with divided attention. He was thinking of Eve and the preceding night.

Feeling bemused and curiously wistful, he reluctantly put aside thoughts of the lovemaking and focused on the discussion that had ended their evening. Maybe he was a stereotypically thickheaded male, but he couldn't understand her. Why, after all these years, was their past involvement still such a viable concern? Before arbitrarily closing the subject, Eve herself had labeled it merely a brief, shallow, even common affair. Not that he agreed with her estimation; involvement with Eve Sheridan, regardless of the degree, could never be termed common. But he had no facts to back up his denial.

Nor could he effectively refute her matter-of-fact contention that any woman would have filled his needs, and she'd just happened to be the first one to catch his eye. Nevertheless, he had carried his baseless argument right up to her doorstep. Not that it got him anywhere, he conceded ruefully. She'd been annoyed and hard put to conceal it.

Frustration lengthened his stride. A sensible man, he kept telling himself that he had no reason to feel guilty. Yet guilt nibbled at his innards like an invasion of sharp-toothed mice.

Amanda's indignant voice jolted him back to the present. "Wait! Wait! You're going too fast, Nate. I can't pick up my shells!"

Chagrined, Nate slowed his steps. "Sorry, sweetheart," he said, stopping entirely as she hunkered beside a ridge of tiny iridescent shells. "What are you going to do with all these shells you're collecting?" he asked, kneeling beside her.

"Make a necklace. See, you can poke holes right here, and put string through the holes and make a necklace."

"You can, hmm?" he said, amused at her earnestness. "You like necklaces, do you?"

"Oh yes. I have five already. See this one?" She lifted the plastic beads hanging on her small chest. "You pull, and it pops loose, and then you just push it back in. Santa Claus brought it for my birthday. It was really Uncle Brian dressed up in a Santa suit," she confided conspiratorily, "but I didn't tell Mommy. Oh look, there's Mommy now!"

Annoyed at the sharp pinch of jealousy that always accompanied Brian Oliver's name, Nate quickly suppressed it.

Something even more disturbing flickered through his mind, but it was lost as he caught sight of Eve.

A dizzying sense of displacement seized him. Nate straightened, his muscles suddenly loose and uncoordinated, his breathing erratic. Watching her stroll toward him heightened his impression of a distortion in time. He knew she wore ankle boots, jeans and a matching shirt. That was sand under her feet. But what he was *seeing* was a skimpily clad nymph dancing across a brightly lighted stage, her long elegant legs and graceful movements mesmerizingly lovely, her wildflower-blue eyes impossibly innocent, her smile provocative, alluring....

The inner vision rapidly expanded. As if someone had flipped a switch, images and memories began rolling across his mind like a running montage.

Vividly he recalled the emotions that had accompanied him to Vegas: the raw, bitter rage he could not conquer, the logic-resistant hurt he despised. As clearly as if it had happened yesterday, he experienced the heart-thrill of meeting Eve and leaving the club with her on his arm, a singular triumph.

He remembered his powerful need to know everything about her. The potent stimulant of her voice filling that need. The slow sweet burn of desire heating his blood, desire he could control as long as they weren't touching.

He felt drunk with remembering.

How hard it had been that first night, leaving her on her doorstep with just a light kiss! He'd told himself it was merely the decent thing to do. And he had to be certain she possessed the sophistication to carry through what those bewitching eyes promised. To his bewilderment, the smile she'd given him when she saw him waiting for her the second night roused every protective male instinct he possessed. She was waitressing, and watching that slender figure support a heavily laden tray had outraged something in him.

As he stood lost in memory, relief and regret mingled in his dark gaze. Relief that he hadn't just taken what he wanted; regret that he had not at least told her why he could offer her nothing except a night or two of pleasure. But his shattered marriage had been too personal and painful to discuss with anyone....

My God, he thought as memories cascaded over his head with drowning force, no wonder she held on to her resentment! He *had* walked out without a backward glance. Because he didn't dare look back, but she hadn't known that. After a night of the most sublime intimacy, he had thanked her for a beautiful weekend and left.

But not before she had demeaned herself—he now *knew* she had felt demeaned—by begging him to stay.

Nate stared down the stretch of dun-colored sand that separated past and present like a transparent curtain. Amanda was running to meet her mother. But he stayed in place, pinned to the spot by the riveting power of recall.

Welling up from forgotten depths, her words stung his ears, bewildered, outraged: *"But I love you! You can't just say goodbye and walk away. I love you!"* With pictorial clarity, he saw himself hugging her, fiercely, furiously. He heard the strain in his indulgent laugh, in his scratchy voice as he coped with her electrifying outburst. What she felt was simple infatuation, he'd said. Something he had to confess to feeling a touch of himself, he'd added lightly, inwardly grimacing as his intense desire for her mocked his words. Wishing things were different, too much the newly soured realist to pretend they were, he had reminded her of the rules laid down at the beginning. Rules made for her protection as well as his peace of mind, he'd stressed defensively.

As he relived the scene again, Nate's heart gave a violent lurch. Eve's stony gaze had glistened with the tears she would not cry.

It would have been so easy to succumb to her appeal. But he knew himself, knew how raw and vulnerable his emotional needs were, how deep his wounds went. If he gave in to his urges, they'd both get hurt.

Even so, leaving her had required an enormous amount of willpower from an all-too-human man.

A smile flitted across his face as he recalled the rest of it. He *hadn't* walked away untouched.

"Nate? Are you okay?"

Eve's concerned voice struck him like a dash of cold water. Totally disoriented, Nate stared at her for a moment. Then time righted itself, and exultation replaced confusion. Eagerness surged through him. He had to tell her he'd regained his memory, that she'd been wrong about him, about everything! He knew it would make a difference. Even the way she looked at him would change. And as for the elusive air of mystery that threatened to drive him right up the wall at times—*finito*, he thought crazily. Over, done with, resolved.

Nate caught himself up short. It would be better to tell her later, when they were alone. Oh, but it was hard to wait! Laughter exploded out of him. Her eyes, her incredible eyes, rounded with puzzlement. He swept her up in his arms and spun her around while she clung to his shoulders and suffered the fusillade of quick little kisses strewn indiscriminately about her person. Even Amanda was amazed.

Abashed, he released the woman and smiled sheepishly at the child. "Nate!" Eve exclaimed, arms akimbo. "What on earth was that all about?"

"Tell you later." Nate felt his mouth stretching wider—he must be grinning like an idiot! Drawing himself up to his full height, he inquired with ponderous dignity, "Shall we go, ladies?"

"We shall," Eve said, adopting his tone. Her smile was especially warm as she took his hand. The tenderness stirring deep within her was for the man, not the child, but it felt very similar.

Amanda took his other hand, and they ran to the car. He made a great ceremony of buckling the tot's seat belt. "Better safe than sorry," he reproved her grumbling dislike of restraining straps. "Little girls don't grow on trees, you know," he added sternly. "Can't go picking them like peaches."

She giggled delightedly, and Eve felt a dangerously invasive softness. The urge to tell him, always present, flared sharply to life. She quelled it with a harsh reminder. If this relationship failed, all sorts of complications could arise over the custody of Amanda. Nathaniel Wright was not a man to give up something he considered his.

Several times during their lovely drive along winding country roads, Nate had to bite his tongue to keep from bursting out with his grand news. He imagined her reaction from numerous different aspects and always with gratifying results.

But he sublimated his urgency in the deeply satisfying pleasure of watching Amanda and Eve enjoy the treat he'd prepared for them. The farm, with its big red barn and white frame house encircled by charming native-stone fences, was warmly inviting. Potted geraniums and rocking chairs adorned the front porch. Eagerly Amanda ran up the grassy path to greet the two beautiful collies waiting there with their middle-aged owners.

"Amanda, wait!" Eve cried, alarmed as the big animals surrounded the little girl. "Nate—"

"They won't hurt her. They're used to small children," Nate said quickly. Taking Eve's arm, he introduced her to the older couple, who were equally quick to reassure her of the dogs' gentle natures.

The smell of new-mown hay permeated the barn. Its dusky
environs offered the seduction of tiny kittens, a fuzzy lamb
born out of season and a frisky tumble of puppies. Shucking
his dignity, Nate sat down on the straw-strewn floor and
plunged into the fun. After checking around for spiders, Eve
joined them.

"Spiders, huh? With me, it's rats. I'm scared to death of the
things," he confided for her ears only. She hugged him.

A pleasant hour or so later, she suggested they take a walk.
"Amanda's getting a little wheezy. Allergies," she explained.
Noting Nate's concerned look, she assured him there was
nothing to worry about. "We keep an inhaler on hand just for
times like this." She nonchalantly handed the small device to
Amanda, who just as casually used it.

Freshly squeezed lemonade sprigged with mint awaited them
when they returned to the house. The tormenting aroma of
homemade pizza hot from the oven and its greedy consump-
tion on an old trestle table in the farmhouse kitchen had
everyone, including Nate, in soaring good spirits. It was worth
every penny, he thought, inhaling gustily as their cheery host-
ess brought in warm peach cobbler dolloped with hand-cranked
ice cream.

Nevertheless, he wasn't at all adverse to leaving the farm. It
was after four when they started back; by then he felt aflame
with anticipation. He was already planning the place and
method to unveil his news—his den. He'd light a crackling fire
and give her pale pink roses and sparkling wine in crystal flutes.
It had to be perfect. Nothing less would do. He meant to speak
his heart tonight.

At the thought, Nate gripped the steering wheel tightly. He
felt as nervous as a kid on the first day of school.

"Nate, this is beautiful," Eve said as she entered the fragrant firelit den. "Champagne? What's the occasion?"

"The occasion," Nate replied, removing her French-blue
cape as if he were unwrapping a gift, "is you and me."

She smiled, a quiet smile. He felt a pinch of undirected anger. She'd laughed and talked freely during their activity-filled
day and romantic evening. But the reserve was empathically

there, and he hated it. He wanted the Eve who dwelled behind its protective folds: the naughty, capricious enchantress of last night, the delicious, violet-eyed fury who'd stormed all over him in the marina parking lot. But she'll be back, he soothed his impatience. Soon.

"Are we going to drink that champagne, or just stand here and look at it?" Eve inquired.

"Hush, wench," he said, causing her eyes to narrow. Capturing her chin, he kissed her as she needed to be kissed, for a long, lovely time.

Flushed and breathless, Eve sank into the deep cushiony couch while he hung up her wrap. His eyes sparkled and a grin shaped his beautiful mouth. She frowned.

"Nate, would you mind telling me why you're looking so smug?"

"All in good time," he said, mystifying her further.

Kneeling, he slipped off the sleek, taupe leather boots sheathing her shapely legs. With them she wore a slender, softly draped wool dress the color of his eyes. "You're one classy lady, lady," he declared, taking in the chignon and pearls completing her ensemble. Then he kissed her again, with gusto and a husky laugh, before tackling the champagne.

With trembling fingers, Eve picked up the two incredibly fragile glasses. Under his expert touch, the cork shot out of the bottle with a satisfying pop, and the pale gold beverage fizzed just enough to tickle the nose nicely.

Savoring the costly bouquet was nearly as pleasing as tasting it. "Umm, this is good. So was dinner. I could get addicted to French cuisine. To you, too, for that matter," she said with a sigh as he sat down beside her.

He smelled wonderful. He tasted even better. Desire shot through her nerve endings as his mouth brushed hers, lightly, lightly, then harder and deeper. Needing to get closer, she leaned toward him until her breasts grazed his chest. His warmth tantalized her nipples into puckered peaks. She slipped her free hand beneath his collar and opened her lips to his tongue.

Coming up for air, Nate buried his face in her perfumed neck until reason returned. *Not yet,* he chided his urge to continue this lovely besiegement of all his senses. He laid his brow against hers and drew a lengthy breath. "Eve, I have a desperate need to know how you feel about me."

His request caught Eve completely unprepared. Rendered speechless, she pulled back and stared at him while the answer hammered like a powerful drumbeat in her ears. She loved him. Not even to herself had she made such a terrifying admission. But she loved him. Utterly, hopelessly.

And senselessly. Only a fool would put herself out on the frail limb of hope without a safety net. She cleared her throat. "I like you, Nate, very much. I also respect and admire you. Believe me, that's very important to a woman. I could never make love with a man I didn't care for. That's why you found me in your bed that night you returned from Portland, not because I was swept off my feet by impulse, but because I made a free, responsible choice to deepen our relationship to intimacy."

It sounded awkward, stilted. He smiled and kissed her nose. "I think it's more than just liking," he challenged softly.

"Nate..." Assailed by battling urges, Eve vented a hard sigh.

"It's all right," he assured her. "I can see your reasoning. 'If he walked out once, he can do it again,' right? I also know the importance of liking and respect. They're part of the bedrock of any real relationship."

She sat back and wet her dry throat with champagne. "Is this one real?"

"This one is very real. It just got delayed a bit, that's all. Because the timing was all wrong. So were you, Eve," he said softly. "Wrong about our affair, wrong about me being a careless man, wrong to think just any woman would have filled my needs. I'd been to Vegas several times before meeting you and gotten along fine without a woman. But I was hooked the minute I laid eyes on you. I had to have you, no matter what the cost. And it did cost. Leaving you that morning was one of the hardest things I've ever done." Nate picked up his own glass and drained it in one swallow. "That's fact, Eve, not supposition."

Although startled by his flat statement, Eve could not immediately pursue it. Her reaction to hearing what she had so often ached to hear was a melting sensation strong enough to crumble vital defenses. Alarm swirled into confusion. "'Fact'? But how do you know that? Unless... Nate, you've remembered!"

It was as much a question as an exclamation. Nate laughed and hugged her. "Yes, I've remembered. This morning, on the beach with Amanda," he said, anticipating her next question. "I don't know what triggered it, but all of a sudden I was seeing you as a gorgeous half-naked redhead instead of a gorgeous, fully clad blonde." He grinned. "You did make a foxy redhead, Miss Sheridan!"

"Well, I—" Her brain was spinning. "They had enough blondes, what they needed were brunettes and redheads, so I chose the latter. But I am a natural blonde," she blurted.

"I know." He chuckled at her pink-cheeked blush. "Anyway, what I said to you last night was solid truth. I was a fouled-up mess, and I knew it. Certainly too fouled-up to risk getting involved with a woman. I knew that, too. But I couldn't resist you, babe, your bright spirit, your gaiety, your sweet warmth. I *needed* you, dammit," he said roughly, then sighed. "At least I had enough sense to make a clean break. But not clean enough. I was miserable, distracted, tempted to turn right around and go back to Vegas... and then that blasted fall happened."

She coughed. "Would you have gone back?"

"I don't know, Eve," he replied, flatly honest. "I do know that I kept having odd feelings about my 'lost weekend' long after it was over. But eventually I convinced myself that it had been just an ordinary holiday and forgot about it. Or so I thought. But that October I bought this beach house for no reason other than that it felt...right. Maybe because here I was close to you, even if I didn't know it."

"Maybe." Warning herself not to put too much stock in that, she stood up and walked to the silver cooler. "More wine?"

"No, thanks. Eve..." Nate paused. He should say this face-to-face, he supposed. But when a man felt as uncertain as he did, it was easier to talk to a woman's back. "I've never believed in love at first sight or even second sight, for that matter. But I do now," he said with an air of reckless abandon. "I love you, Eve Sheridan."

His words washed over Eve like a towering wave, leaving in its wake a stunningly painful joy. Turning to confront his alert dark eyes increased the lump in her throat. She swallowed, but it wouldn't go away. Her gaze met his in mute appeal. Two strides brought him to her side, and her into his arms.

"I know I behaved badly when you said those same words to me," he murmured ruefully.

She half groaned. "You remember that, too?"

"Oh yes, I remember. I still don't know if you were serious. But I am. I want a future with you, Eve. I want you to be part of my life. The best part," he appended with a tender smile.

This time his words threw her into total panic. Oh God, she thought with an edge of hysteria, I haven't even *told* him yet! "Nate, I don't know what to say, I..." She inhaled, a deep gulp of air that did nothing to clear her head. "It's too soon—too much is happening too soon. It's only been a month."

"It was four years last April," he corrected dryly. "But I see your point." The shoulders he held in a death grip relaxed. He kissed her trembling lips. "Think about it if you need to." His mouth pressed harder. "We've got plenty of time."

So sweet, she thought, aching to reveal her love. But the rejected words she'd spoken once before lay in a tangled snarl at the back of her throat. Blindly setting aside her glass, she gave herself to him, her lips opening to his in sweet surrender. His hands slid under her skirt, and she forgot to think.

In his bedroom, they undressed without speaking, but during the rapturous interlude that followed, she heard, for the first time, words of affection uttered in his deepest, huskiest voice. She didn't reciprocate; the tyranny of caution kept a lock on her own treasure chest of love words. But Nate didn't seem to mind.

It was only later, as they were saying good-night on her porch, that he put any pressure on her. Curving one arm around her waist, he drew her close and tilted up her face. "Eve, I have to know. Do you love me?"

Oh yes, I love you! she thought. But she wasn't able to say it just yet. Just acknowledging it to herself made her feel nakedly vulnerable. Her fingertips glided caressingly across his mouth. "You know I do. Now unhand me and go home. I'm exhausted," she accused.

To her relief Nate laughed and left her with his brand stamped firmly on her mouth.

Wearily she climbed the stairs to her bedroom. As tired as she was, she still had some thinking to do. Staying awake long enough to do it shouldn't pose much of a problem, she thought as she approached the bed. For Amanda was sleeping with her, and Amanda slept crossways, sideways, upside-downways; any way she could get, she got, and her feet were everywhere and mostly on Eve.

With amused tolerance, Eve accepted the discomfort. Maybe it would help keep her eyelids open. They felt like lead.

Cuddling up to the warm little body, she tried to sort through her contradictory emotions. The beauty of a cherished dream coming true was hedged with fear; it was dangerous to feel so happy. And while the possibility of being Nate's wife elated her, it also evoked a murky sense of apprehension she couldn't explain and was too sleepy to try.

Guilt plagued her. Tonight's receptive intimacy had provided an excellent opportunity to tell Nate he was a father. Perversely, she had blocked logic's nudges. Vexed, she told herself that guilt was uncalled for. It had only been a few weeks—far too early for such momentous decisions. Snuggling deeper into the comforter's warmth, she closed her eyes, her muscles fluidly relaxed. There was no need to rush into anything.

She had time.

Three in the morning. Muttering an oath, Nate pulled on his trousers and strode out to his private deck. He had taken Eve home hours ago, and should, by all rights, be sleeping soundly. Instead he'd tossed and turned in a hot welter of sheets that still bore her elusive scent. *Elusive*. Yeah, that's it, he thought, pacing. After all that had occurred between them, all the explanatory words, the earthshaking declaration—the baring of his soul, for God's sake—she was still just as elusive, still just as mysterious as the day he'd met her on the beach.

He walked to the rail and stared at the ocean. The night was so black that its waters glowed with a faint florescence. With a twist of heart, he recalled Eve's soft voice, barely audible over the swish of undulating waves. *"You know I do."* Not very strong assurance for a man whose deepest need was to know himself loved and wanted beyond a shadow of doubt, he thought ironically. Well, thank God she did return his affections. She was the soul mate he'd been looking for all his adult life.

Jamming his hands into his pockets, he began pacing again, the sound of his bare feet a dull thud on the wooden floor. Something else was gnawing at his mind. What?

Deliberately relaxing, he let his mind drift back through the day. Eve, breathtakingly lovely in her leotard, pink cheeked under his admiring scrutiny. Amanda, on the beach, collecting shells for a necklace. She liked necklaces, he remembered, smiling. With an inner eye, he saw her holding out her brightly colored beads for his admiration, heard the endearing pride in her sweet voice. *"Santa Claus brought it for my birthday...."*

Nate stopped dead, his brow knitting into a puzzled frown. A Christmas birthday?

Eleven

"Hannah, it's nine o'clock already. Why on earth didn't you wake me?" Eve asked testily.

"You were up till the wee hours of the morning," Hannah shot back, dark eyes snapping. "You'd have looked like a hollow-eyed witch if I'd'a awoken you earlier."

"God forbid that I look like a hollow-eyed witch," Eve said with a sigh, none too sure she didn't. "Well, hi, honey!" she exclaimed as Mary Jo came in. "Where have you been?"

"I ran out to the store." Stopping to pick up the little girl dogging her footsteps, Mary Jo perched on the bed. "So, why were you up and about till the wee hours, cousin? The usual tall, dark and handsome reason?"

"No. Well, maybe some. But mostly it was Amanda. I should have guessed she wasn't feeling well when I found her in my bed last night. An asthma attack. A pretty bad one. I had to put her on the nebulizer," Eve said, referring to the portable breathing machine she'd purchased to help relieve Amanda's distress. "She still has a bit of an audible rale, but she's much better, hmm, baby? You're an angel, Hannah." She sighed as the housekeeper brought in a pot of coffee and two bowls of what Hannah referred to as "disgusting gloop"— cottage cheese sprinkled with raisins, sunflower seeds and shredded coconut, a confection both cousins found seductively delicious.

Taking Amanda firmly in hand, Hannah left the two young women to their breakfasts. Mary Jo poured the coffee.

"Seen Patrick lately?" she asked.

"No. I guess he's been busy with that piracy case," Eve replied, matching her casual tone. "Why?"

"Just curious." Daintily Mary Jo bit the end off a croissant. "I can't eat too much—I have a luncheon date with the editor of our local paper. So how goes it with you and Nate?"

Eve's tender smile wavered. Her new relationship with Nate was still too unsettling to discuss with ease. She savored a bite of gloop. "Progressing. He regained his memory yesterday, on the beach with Amanda, of all places. He waited until last night to tell me about it. Then he...told me he loved me and wanted a future together," she ended in a rush.

Sorting through appropriate responses, Mary Jo chose one that fit the look in her cousin's eyes. "How did you react?"

"Sheer and utter panic."

"I see. You love him, he loves you, he proposes a future together, which is exactly what you want—and you panic. Perfectly natural reaction."

Smiling at her cousin's droll conclusion, Eve defended, "Well, it was. I felt like I was on a runaway train. Besides, I haven't even told him about Amanda yet."

"I guessed that much. But Eve, he does have to be told."

"I'm aware of that, Mary Jo," Eve replied with a trace of irritation. "But it's going to be a hard thing to do. And knowing he loves me doesn't make it any easier. What if he stops, what then? I'm not afraid for myself—it's Amanda I can't risk. If our relationship failed, where would she end up? Six months here and six months there? Weekends with Daddy, weekdays with Mommy, split holidays?" She gave a little shudder, then grimaced as she met perceptive brown eyes. "I guess what I'm looking for is a guarantee, and there aren't any. But that doesn't keep me from wanting one."

"I know. But it seems to me that if you want him, sooner or later you're going to have to take a chance."

"Sooner or later." A small silence ensued before Eve continued on a brighter note. "I've still got dibs on that seascape I like so much."

"It's on display at the gallery right now, but when the show's over, it's yours, come what may. From me to you, with love."

"Thank you," Eve said, deciding not to sully the splendid gift with protestations. "That particular painting means a lot to me." She reached for a croissant. "What exciting things have you been up to?"

Mary Jo accepted the shift of subjects with the same tender grace. They went through two pots of coffee before she finished relating what she'd been doing. By then the day had decided upon its weather—flannel gray, with gusty winds.

Just as well, Eve thought. Since the day after an asthmatic episode was always filled with quiet indoor activities for Amanda, canceling the picnic would be easier than expected.

"We'll do it tomorrow," Nate said when she called him. "It'll have cleared up by then. You didn't tell me Amanda has asthma. Just allergies, you said."

"Her type of asthma is brought on by allergies."

"Which were brought on by her visit to the farm. Why didn't you say something, Eve? I feel responsible for her illness."

"I'm the only one responsible for Amanda." The automatic reply provoked a hard inner sigh; his concern should be appreciated, not resented. "The only thing you're to blame for is the lovely time she had," she continued on a softer note. "And the reason I didn't say anything before is because, well, as much as I'd like to, I can't wrap her in cotton batting, not if she's to lead a normal life. Fortunately she gets over these attacks quickly and usually feels fine in a day or so. Meantime, would you like to have lunch with us, maybe rent a movie?"

"Fine with me. Noon?"

His reply was rather terse, she thought. "Yes. But Nate, if you have something better to do, which wouldn't have to be all that much," she added with a dry chuckle, "I'll understand."

"The only other thing I have on my schedule is a dinner engagement tonight. It's business, but you'll get a great meal out of it. I've made reservations at Cables."

"You didn't say anything about a business dinner last night."

"I didn't know about it last night. Honi just got into town an hour or so ago—"

"Honi?" Eve interrupted sharply, and wished she hadn't.

"Honi Preston of Preston Computer Marts, remember? Strictly business, remember? And you're included, so what's the problem?" he asked irritably.

With effort, Eve kept her tone mild. "None. Except that I won't be there. You're not in too good of a mood this morning, are you?"

Nate expelled a long breath. "Sorry, sweetheart," he said gruffly. "I guess I am feeling a bit cranky...." His voice rose. "What do you mean, you won't be there?"

"Amanda's still a little wheezy, so I think I'd better stick around here tonight. One of the penalties of parenthood. But you enjoy your dinner. Oh, Mary Jo came in this morning, brimming over with excitement, as usual. She's been giving all sorts of interviews and going to fancy receptions. Plus, three of her paintings have already sold, and she hasn't even had her show yet! By the way, you don't happen to need a four-wheel-drive vehicle, do you? She's selling her Blazer. I know she hates to part with it, but every little bit helps, I guess," Eve chattered on, trying to mask her unruly emotions.

"I already have one," Nate said shortly. "Eve, I'm sorry you won't be joining us for dinner tonight—you know I want you there with me. But I'm not going to feel guilty about dining alone with another woman."

"There's no reason you should," she snapped.

"No, there isn't. Not if you trust me."

She twisted the telephone cord around her fingers, then let it go. "I do. I trust you to have a miserable time and miss me terribly. Now, what do you want for lunch—tuna or grilled cheese?"

"Those are my choices?" he asked with a mock groan.

"That's it. Another penalty of parenthood," she quipped.

He laughed. "I'll keep that in mind. Can I bring anything?"

"A small appetite," she suggested puckishly. "You can make up for it tonight at Cables. See you around noon."

Replacing the receiver, Eve stared into the grayness outside her window. Nervously she wondered if inviting him for lunch and a Disney video was such a good idea, after all. They'd been so strained with each other, and sensitive female antennae had picked up on the tension in him even over the telephone....

"Now don't go getting all flitter nerved just because he was a little cranky," Mary Jo advised when Eve aired her doubts. "Everyone gets up on the wrong side of the bed now and then. I'm sure that's all it is."

"You're probably right," Eve agreed, and went on to the kitchen knowing full well she'd be a flitter-nerved mess by the time he was due to arrive.

When he did come striding in the door, she had to chide herself for being too sensitive. He kissed her, greeted Hannah nicely and complimented Amanda on her attire, which consisted of Eve's suede pumps and tunic dragging around her heels, Mary Jo's gardening hat and five strands of assorted beads.

"You look pretty good, too," he told Eve, eyeing with sensual appreciation the clove-pink sweater and slacks hugging her curvaceous form.

Eve's cheeks matched her sweater as she responded to his intimate smile. She reached up to brush back his hair and let her hand linger a moment before directing him to the kitchen.

In his opinion, grilled-cheese sandwiches and a chocolate sheet cake whipped up by Hannah made a splendid luncheon. He even liked Disney movies, Eve thought, watching his performance with a covert smile. It was almost as if he were trying to impress her. If so, he was succeeding. Contentment settled over her like a warm shawl. They sat on the couch, fingers linked, shoulders touching. Amanda lay on the carpet on her stomach, feet waving over her bottom. Outside, patches of fog ghosted around the windows; inside, a fire snapped and crackled in the corner fireplace, and the smell of spiced tea filtered in from the kitchen. Opening to the fullest every sense she possessed, Eve knew moments of pure happiness.

But he left around three, and the fire went out, and the tea grew cold. While Hannah and Amanda settled down for a nap, Eve wrapped up in an afghan and sat on the sheltered deck listening to the sea. She would put Nate and Honi's business dinner into proper perspective if it took all night.

Warm sunlight bathed the land when Eve came downstairs the next morning. Amanda awoke feeling so full of herself that her exasperated mother sent her outside to play until Nate arrived.

Just the sight of him striding up the walk, a tall vibrant man clad in lean gray cords and knit shirt, sent Eve's heartbeat into a joyous new rhythm. Contrarily, an icy vein of fear ran with her excitement. Loving him had left her prey to the terrible pain of losing him again. Her greeting kiss was brief but fierce.

They picnicked on his deck. Nate served grilled chicken and pasta salad, which Amanda ate, although she much preferred peanut butter.

"Guess I'm going to have to update my larder," Nate mused. "How the heck do you know what kids want to eat, anyway?"

"You ask them. Then you balance their answers with what *you* want them to eat." Eve removed the slice of water chestnut Amanda was regarding with deep suspicion and ate it herself. "By the way, how did you and Honi get along last night? Accomplish anything constructive?" she asked, wrinkling her nose.

"We got along just fine," he replied with noticeable satisfaction. "Preston Computer Marts will carry my entire line in return for exclusive distributorship rights to my new data retrieval program. A mutually agreeable business deal made, as many others will be, over a dinner table."

"Congratulations!" Eve said, and raised her glass to him.

"Thank you." They touched glasses. His keen gray eyes regarded her measuringly. "You're really not bothered by that dinner with Honi?"

"No," Eve replied, more or less truthfully. What bothered her was the odd intensity she glimpsed in his eyes and heard as an undertone in his rich voice. She'd caught traces of it yesterday. Her certainty wavered as he gave her a warm smile of approval and resumed eating. You're overreacting again, Eve, she chided her current anxiety attack. After all, their relationship had undergone a radical change, and they were still trying to find their footing. Naturally they'd feel a little awkward with each other.

Just then he caught her eye with a lusty wink, and a rush of pleasure spread through her. Quelling her fuzzy doubts, she resolved to stop analyzing and just enjoy.

After lunch they drove inland, stopping here and there, exploring, discovering wild apple trees and a placid stream with equal pleasure. With a patience that warmed the heart, Nate began teaching Amanda the ancient art of skipping stones across a stream. Eve settled down on the leafy bank, content to watch and listen, her mood quietly reflective.

Amanda's health problems had made the little girl shy and wary of strangers, but with Nate she was her delightful self, unwary and outgoing, as if she knew she could trust this big soft-spoken man. Which is more than I can say for myself, Eve thought, her mouth twisting in self-chastisement. It's easy to love. Trusting's the hard part. Trusting and forgetting.

"A penny for your thoughts," Nate offered, sitting down beside her.

"Cheapskate." Loving his rumbling laugh, she moved into the muscled warmth of his shoulder. "Such a beautiful day." She sighed luxuriously. It was October now, and autumn had set the countryside ablaze with its brilliant foliage. The air she breathed had a marvelous tang, and the sky was flawlessly blue. A few feet away, the long graceful fronds of an enormous weeping willow swept the grass with every breeze, a wind chime of loveliness. Its secretive depths could have sheltered a unicorn, she thought whimsically. She felt wistfully happy and a little nostalgic, too.

"It'll be odd getting up and going to work Monday, instead of being with you. That's such a nice way to begin the morning," she said with another sigh.

"I can think of a nicer one," he murmured, nuzzling her ear.

Their soft laughter was the essence of intimacy.

His arms curled around her midriff. "How long did you stay in Vegas after I left?"

He spoke idly. Relaxing, she replied with humorous self-mockery, "Just long enough to cry my broken heart out. I was pretty disillusioned with Vegas by then, so I just went home." Tipping back her head, she looked up at him. "Why do you ask?"

"Just wondering. Despite all that's happened between us, you're still my mysterious Eve. I'll probably grow old and gray trying to figure *you* out," he growled.

Her low, pleased laugh evoked a frown before he burned a quick kiss on her lips. Shifting into a more comfortable position, Eve closed her eyes to the sun's caressing heat.

"Tell me what you're thinking," he said, breaking the languid silence.

"I was thinking about tomorrow and all of us going our separate ways. You to Portland, Amanda and me back to Concord, Mary Jo to New York, Patrick to...where, exactly?" she asked, diverted by curiosity.

"He's got an old farm about ten miles from my place," Nate replied. Although Patrick's shares of Wright Enterprises had made him wealthy, he was fiercely devoted to his three hundred acres of hardscrabble land. "His crops cost more to grow than to buy at market, but he doesn't seem to mind."

"That sounds just like Patrick!" Eve said approvingly. She sobered as the same soft, mixed-up wistfulness invaded her amusement. "I'm going to miss him when I leave. So will Mary Jo. We had our fun, didn't we, the four of us?" Her gaze mapped his rugged features. "I'm going to miss you, too, Nathaniel Wright," she murmured. "I'm going to miss you very much."

A dark eyebrow winged up. "Maybe I'm becoming paranoid about you, but to the untrained ear, that sounded curiously much like, 'Goodbye, it's been fun, give me a call sometime,'" he observed.

"'Untrained ear' is right," she sniffed, grateful that he'd provided a way to ease into talk of the future. "You know darn well I'll be counting the seconds until you show up on my doorstep again.'' Mock-serious, she frowned at him. ''You are going to show up, aren't you?''

''I imagine I will, Elizabeth Eve,'' he drawled. ''I'm leaving Tuesday for a software show in California, but I'll be back Friday night. Which means I'll be seeing you Saturday, one week from today. You can count on that.''

''I am,'' she said simply.

Nate smiled his reply. Amanda was wandering around gathering snips of asters and goldenrod. Watching her, he mused, ''Must be a funny feeling, knowing you're shaping a human being. Like an artist working with living clay. Makes me wish...''

''What?''

''I don't know. That I was an artist, perhaps.'' His mouth formed a gentle curve. ''You've done a fine job of creating, Eve.''

''Thank you,'' Eve said, and averted her gaze as the urge to confide in him collided with unyielding caution.

''You're welcome,'' he responded with that beguiling trace of formality, then got up to answer Amanda's urgent summons. She'd found an empty bird's nest and had to have it.

Still beset with dueling urges, Eve glanced down at her ringless left hand, an effective reminder that love didn't always lead to marriage. Shivering, she waited until he had collected the small nest before coming to her feet. ''Nate, let's start home now, its getting chilly,'' she called.

''Coming! Want a ride, princess?'' he inquired of Amanda.

''What did you call her?'' Eve asked, more sharply than intended.

''Princess.'' Nate set the little girl on his shoulders. His eyes narrowed. ''Is that another no-no?''

''No, of course not. It's just that, well, that was my father's nickname for me,'' Eve replied lamely. ''It startled me, that's all, hearing you call *her* princess.'' Laughing, she patted the bouncing little fanny astride Nate's broad shoulders. ''How's the view up there, kiddo?''

''Fan-tastic!'' Amanda removed a hand from Nate's hair and waved it with her merry response. The hint of tension vanished under shared laughter.

She fell asleep on the drive home. Nate seemed to be absorbed in some private introspection, so Eve, too, drowsed through the dusky miles.

Patrick's car was parked in the driveway. Apparently he had just arrived; he was opening the gate when they drove up. Leaving Amanda to Nate, Eve got out and walked around the car.

"Hi, Patrick! Where have you been keeping yourself? I've missed you," she accused with a genuine rush of affection.

"Been hither and yon, mostly yon," came Patrick's laconic answer. "You can kiss me if you want, but don't get carried away. Nate's watching, and you know what a temper he has."

"Oh, Patrick!" Laughing, she flung her arms around him and kissed his cheek. "What are you doing here, anyway?" she asked, then made a moue at her tactlessness.

Unperturbed, he ruffled her hair. "I was looking for Nate, and when I didn't find him at home, I figured the next best place to look was here." His Irish-blue gaze shifted to the man who was lifting a drowsy-eyed Amanda from the car. "Hello, Nate! Who's your sleepy friend? Wouldn't be little Miss Sheridan herself, would it?"

"It would," Eve answered. Wondering how much Nate had told him, she continued proudly, "Patrick, my daughter, Amanda."

"Well, hi, cutie-pie," Patrick said, and received a flirtatious under-the-lashes smile. "Lord, Lord, if she's not gonna drive some poor man crazy someday!" he said to Nate.

"Like mother, like daughter," Nate murmured.

"Huh!" Eve snorted, absurdly pleased, and took her grubby little daughter inside to Hannah. "A good soak, then an early supper and bedtime," she instructed. "Is Mary Jo around?"

"She's having dinner with friends," Hannah said.

Relieved, Eve walked back outside in time to wave goodbye to Patrick. Nate was leaning against his car, his face expressionless as he watched her approach. Something fluttered wildly in her stomach.

"I forgot to ask what we're doing tonight," she said.

"Whatever you want."

Gauging his quiet voice, she felt a sudden strong need to see laughter and excitement lighting up his deep gray eyes. She knew how much he valued spontaneity. So be spontaneous, she jabbed at herself. "Well, dinner, of course. But first I want a long hot shower. I imagine you do, too—" the tip of her tongue tucked into a mischievous grin "—so I thought we could take one together. Conserve water that way," she explained gravely.

"A fine argument for communal bathing," Nate agreed with a smile as dry as alum. His sexy, sparkling-eyed sorceress was back, and he knew he couldn't resist her bewitchery. But he wanted to.

Eve walked into his bedroom with the air of one who owned it. She had delayed their departure only long enough to change her jeans for a simple shift. Skimming it over her head, she tossed the cotton garment on a chair and sauntered to the bathroom. Nate was undressing. She ignored the powerful torso emerging from concealment the way she would ignore a fire in her kitchen.

Carelessly she pinned her hair atop her head. She turned on the shower and stepped into it. Lathering, she wondered what detained him.

When the shower door did swish open, Nate simply stared at her for a moment. She stood under a misty waterfall, her body wet and gleaming, the golden down of her womanhood bejeweled with clinging droplets. "My God," he whispered reverently.

Suddenly shy, Eve gave a throaty laugh. "You're just in time," she said. "I need someone to scrub my back."

Taking the pale blue bar she held out, he closed the door and slowly began soaping her back. He took a long time to work his way down the tender curve of hips to the delicacy of her ankles.

Kneeling, he watched the water erase his frothy white handiwork. Rising, he glided his hands over her sleek legs, upward to mounded hillocks, caressing, moving on. A nest of wet silk had formed at her nape. He tasted it, then stitched a trail of kisses across her tawny shoulders.

His lips were cool fire on her hot skin. Eve quivered as his hands slid under her arms to cup her breasts. He held her so for a moment, his hard warmth pressed deep into pliant curves. "God, I can't resist you," he muttered thickly.

"Do you want to resist?" she murmured.

"Sometimes." He nipped her shoulder. "But you cast a wicked spell, Eve."

"So do you." She turned, her smile as sultry as her voice. Languidly she began soaping his chest, enjoying the contrast of white lather on bronzed skin and dark coarse hair. He was tremendously aroused, his eyes smoldering with the excitement she felt flowing from him. It passed through her like a tingling shock of electricity.

Water streamed down his taut frame. He stepped from under the shower head and pulled her with him. They kissed with avid hunger. She felt his hands move to her hips in a sleek, sensuous glide. His mouth edged lower, sending erotic pulses of pleasure through her erect nipples. Her eyes closed. The soap slid from her fingers. There was only Nate, his smell, his rough warm mouth, the fiery bloom of desire swelling within her.

Opening the door, he stepped out, half lifting her, and lowered her to the carpet. Her eyes flew wide in question. Laughing deeply, he eased down to her. "This is ridiculous and it's all your fault!" he charged, fitting his long frame to hers.

Incredulous, Eve stared at him. The bathroom proper was small and narrow. Although she fit nicely into her allotted space, he was too tall, too big—they would surely kill themselves in this object-lined nook, she thought wildly. His mouth found hers, his slick body making a swift sensual adjustment. And then he found what he sought, and Eve's power to think simply ebbed away on a tide of rapture.

It was surely ridiculous. It was most certainly wonderful. Drifting down from impossible heights, Eve nuzzled the shoulder that smothered her. The bath mat was biting into her skin. But they were entangled in a lovely snarl of limbs, and she didn't dare make an incautious movement.

"Nathaniel," she said sadly, "I think my back is breaking. I think I also feel a few bruises starting up."

He sighed. "I think I've dislocated something or other my-self. Could be something important, too.... Stop that and help me untangle us. Gently, if you please?"

Eve giggled. It was all right, she thought with a sudden sense of relief that defied reason.

With careful maneuvering, Nate regained his footing and helped her up. They showered again, but this time he carried her to the bed before things got out of hand.

"Let's talk, Eve," he said abruptly, rolling onto his back.

"Later." Eve leaned over him and let her towel-damp hair flow across his chest. "Much later." She kissed his firm mouth, marveling at the unplumbed depths of her sexuality. "It can wait, can't it?" she coaxed sweetly.

"No, it can't wait." Nate exerted pressure on her shoulders while she laughed and protested, bearing her down until her bewildered eyes met his determined gaze. "It's time, Eve. Past time, in fact. Long past time."

His face was as stern as his voice. "Nate, I don't under-stand. Time for what?" Eve asked, struggling to calm the pan-icky awareness of something gone terribly wrong.

"Time you told me that I'm Amanda's father."

Twelve

Had Nate been less alert, he would have missed the impact his demand had upon her. The panic and confusion darkening her lovely eyes like a cloud-shadow was swiftly gone. Frowning, she slowly let her head fall back upon the pillow.

"What on earth makes you think that?" she asked, incredulous.

He stared at her, grudging admiration tinging his disbelief as she steadily met his gaze. "I might have known the element of surprise wouldn't work with you," he said finally. "But the innocent act won't work with me, either. I know, Eve."

"You know what?" she asked, annoyed at his persistence.

"That Amanda's my daughter."

"Then you know nothing. Amanda's *my* daughter."

Eve listened to her hostile response with a despairing sense of inadequacy. Stop reacting and start thinking! an inner voice screamed. But the defenses she'd built against Nate refused to yield to reason. Acting on blind instinct, she protested, "Nate, this is crazy. I told you about my high school sweetheart, how

I went home to him after you left me in Vegas. My goodness, I can't imagine where you got the idea that *you* were her father!''

"You can't, huh? Well, that much is probably true.'' Nate's grating laugh clawed at his throat, adding to the pain her words inflicted. He hungered for her admission, but he didn't really need it. To his decisive mind, her very evasiveness was confirming what he'd tried so desperately to deny. Their whole relationship was built on a network of lies.

He felt like a volcano on the verge of eruption.

With rigid discipline, he pushed away from her, stood up and put on his navy robe, then tossed her a terry-cloth kimono. "Put that on, will you?'' he requested tightly. "You're a distraction I can damn well do without right now.''

Her eyes flashed, but she complied. Facing him, she knotted the sash with a toss of head that denied the weakness of trembling fingers. She waited, shoulders thrown back, her gaze wary and alert. Nate clenched his hands so hard his knuckles whitened. Despite her fighter's stance, she looked incredibly small and fragile in the heavy white garment. Dispassion, he reminded himself. But the hand he raked through his hair was savagely at odds with his quiet voice.

"Let's try a little more of that truth, shall we?'' he suggested. "Maybe even inject a few solid facts, such as Amanda's Christmas birthday.''

She stared. "Her Christmas birthday?''

"Yes, Eve. Amanda told me, that day on the beach...the day my memory returned.'' Nate hesitated as more pieces of his maddening puzzle fell into place. "That's what triggered my recall. And my conclusions, too, I suppose, although that wasn't so sudden. I'd begun having these odd little feelings about your story before then, but I refused to credit my hunches. They were too insane, too demeaning to the proud, honest woman I admired so much.''

His sarcasm propelled her chin higher. He balled his hands into fists again.

"Even when Amanda told me that Santa brought her birthday presents—Santa being dear Uncle Brian, of course,'' he growled, stabbed with jealousy at the thought of another man having that fatherly privilege, "even then there was still some doubt. I kept telling myself you *could* have gone straight home after I left Vegas. I mean, you said it yourself—you were hurt, disillusioned, you needed consolation and you found it. I could understand. I'd felt that kind of raw need before...." Struggling for control, he rammed his aching fingers into his pockets. "Deceiving myself to that extent wasn't easy, but it was more palatable than the alternative."

"What alternative is that?" she asked, as if listening to an interesting discourse.

"That you lied to me," he said softly through his teeth. "Deliberately, continuously, looked me in the face and lied. Don't shake your head—the facts are there, dammit! The very first thing you told me about Amanda was a lie! You said she'd just turned three, when in reality she was nearly four. Count backwards nine months from December and you get April, which is when we met, exactly four years and nine months ago. Even you can't twist those kind of facts around."

Eve felt as if she were standing in quicksand. If she struggled, she'd only sink faster. But she still struggled. "Sometimes facts themselves can be deceptive, Nate," she countered. She shrugged off the robe and reached for her shift. "Look, I've told you about Bax, and I don't intend to repeat myself." The loose frock flowed down her golden form. "I'm tired, I'm hungry, and if you want to carry on with this, fine, but you can do it alone. I'm going home."

She risked a step.

Nate's hand whipped out and caught her arm. "Oh, stop it, Eve!" he exploded. "There was no Bax, no shattered romance, no 'disinterested' other man!"

"No, you're wrong, Nate, there was another man...." Eve floundered, her wits scattering as she met eyes as cold and blank as slate. *Oh, Amanda!* Assailed from within and without, she jerked her arm free and sat down on the bed. "I never lied to you," she insisted doggedly. "I was vague about Amanda's age, yes, but I didn't lie. Bax was, and is, a very real person."

Glancing at the red marks on her arm, Nate swore and turned away from the hurtful sight. "I'll grant you his existence. But it's my child you were carrying." Her stubborn silence provoked him to another oath. "Eve, for God's sake, just admit it? When you left Vegas you were pregnant!"

"All right, damn you, I was *pregnant!* Pregnant and desperate!"

Her words seemed to ring on and on in the starkly quiet room. Calm down, she warned herself. But a glance at Nate deepened the hot prickly anxiety hollowing out her chest. His back was stiff with unspent anger. It accused her.

"Desperate and scared and *alone*," she added with devastating softness.

"I'm aware of that," he replied tonelessly.

"I had no way to reach you. No address, no telephone number, not even so much as the name of the company you worked for."

"I know that, too. I accept my full share of blame for the mess we've made of it. But the past doesn't excuse the present." He wheeled, his eyes dark pits in his shadowed face. "All the hours we spent together this past month, all the opportunities you had to tell me! We've been friends, we've been lovers. I even proposed a future together. But still you kept silent. Why? Amanda's my daughter, too."

My daughter. Nate paused, momentarily distracted by the feeling that rolled over him as abstract words suddenly assumed physical shape and meaning. It was unlike anything he'd ever experienced. Outrage joined the volatile mix of hurt and betrayal and roared into a furious question. "How the *hell* could you keep something like this to yourself?"

"Because I wasn't ready to reveal it, that's why," Eve replied reasonably, but the flags of temper were flying high in her cheeks. "I didn't know what kind of man you were. In fact, I wasn't sure you were even worthy of meeting Amanda, much less knowing she was yours. Surely you can see why I—"

"I do see why. But I also gave *you* every chance to see. To see that I wasn't a monster, that I was worthy of trust, that I was decent, dammit!"

Catching himself up short, Nate strode to the fireplace and leaned against the mantel. *Take it easy, man. You can't afford to go off half-cocked,* he admonished his unstable self. But

God, he was hurting! The pain rode roughshod over his reason.

"Or didn't that matter to you? Maybe I'm overlooking something here, like what you really want. That's it, isn't it?" he asked with an air of discovery. "I could've gone on proving myself until I was blue in the face and it wouldn't have made any difference, because you never intended telling me. I mean, why bother when you could have it all—my daughter, me, my money—without taking a single risk? And if that clever scheme didn't work, there was always Brian Oliver to fall back on, so why not go for it?" he forged on, hurling out every half-baked idea that raged through his mind. "Either way, you'd come out a winner."

Eve clenched her jaw until her teeth hurt. His ugly charge was a stinging affront to all the nights she'd wept over him. Him, not his money—she didn't give a damn about his money! Or him now, either, for that matter, she thought bitterly, as if bitterness would blunt the terrible ache of love.

"I'm not going to dignify that with a denial," she said, grimly composed. "So. Now that we know what you think of me, what next, Nate?"

"I want my child. And I will have her, even if it means a legal battle."

Legal battle! Eve covered her involuntary gasp with a rusty cough. "Nate..." She swallowed, and tried again. "You know you have no grounds for a legal battle, not a shred of proof that she's yours. You'd be laughed out of any court in the land. You couldn't possibly gain custody of Amanda!"

"But I can give it one hell of a try."

His soft, steely voice sliced to the maternal quick of her soul. "Nate, I'm warning you," she said in a rising voice.

"And I'm warning you. I've got a right to claim my daughter, and I'll exercise that right to the fullest."

"A right? You dare talk to me of *rights*?" Eve shot to her feet in a blaze of defensive fury. "Where were you when I was laboring for eighteen hours to bring her into the world? Where were you when I brought her home, scared to death, a new mother who didn't have the foggiest idea of how to cope! And where were you when I sat rocking a feverish baby throughout many a long night? What were you doing while I paced a hospital corridor and wondered if she'd make it this time!''

Nate's mouth opened, but a slashing hand shut out anything he might say.

"And that precious money you're so concerned about—where was it when I was wondering how I was going to pay for her medicines, her constant office visits, all those little expenses that insurance doesn't cover? Special nurses? *I* provided them. Breathing machines for asthma attacks? *I* bought them. Special shoes for Amanda, food and clothes and shelter? Guess who?'' she invited caustically. "I've earned the right to be called Mommy. But what on earth makes you think you have a right to be called Daddy?''

"Because I am.''

"Biologically, yes. But that's all,'' she said, ignoring his ragged tone. "Now get out of here. I've had enough of you for one evening. Don't touch me, Nate,'' she warned as he stepped toward her. "I don't want your hands on me. I don't even want to look at you! Just get out of here and leave me alone!''

Because he wanted to cry, and grown men didn't cry, he laughed. "I'd be glad to oblige you, Eve, if this weren't my house.''

"Oh!'' She looked around in confusion. "In that case, I'll leave.'' Slipping on her shoes, she hurried to the foyer and snatched up her jacket and purse.

Beyond words, feeling cheated and betrayed and heavily in the wrong, he followed.

She paused at the door for a final warning. "I know you're a powerful man, Nate, and used to getting your own way. But not this time, not with Amanda. I'd advise you to think twice before you take me on, because I can be a hellcat where she's concerned.''

Eyes shimmering with unshed tears, she stood tall and proud, an arrow aimed straight at his heart. Nate deflected it with the hot unthinking rage of a man unjustly accused. "And I'd advise you to get a good lawyer. I already have one.''

Her mouth twisted. "Of course you have. Good night, Nate. Do sleep well.'' She opened the door, stepped outside and was swallowed up by the night.

A classy exit, Nate admitted. His shoulders sagged. It would be a long time before he slept well.

Nearly a week later, Eve made her way through the crowded exercise studio and hurried outside. She left the sidewalk and took the grassy shortcut to staff parking. Leaves rustled underfoot. Although an abundance still clung to the trees, sunset-hued drifts carpeted the gentle slope she climbed. She would have enjoyed the brisk autumn day, had she not lost the capacity for joy.

Brian passed by as she got into her car. He knew about Nate. To an excess, very likely, she thought with a soft smile. He was a good listener. With a jaunty salute, Eve drove onto the street.

Her thoughts inevitably led to Nate. Her mind winged back to the night they had parted. She remembered his smile as he bid her farewell, a strange, sad, cynical curve of mouth that squeezed her heart unmercifully. By the time she had reached Mary Jo's cottage, she was shaking all over.

"Perfectly natural reaction," she muttered, turning onto her street. "My loveliest dream and my worst nightmare, both one and the same."

She stopped the car in her driveway and sat there for a moment. Whoops of glee resounded from the fenced backyard. Amanda was destroying the pile of leaves raked up by a laughing Mary Jo.

"Hey, honey!" Mary Jo shouted. "Here, Mandy, you rake awhile. Mommy and I need to have a little talk."

"Hey, yourself," Eve returned. Opening the gate, she accepted a juicy kiss from Amanda, then arched an eyebrow. "What are we talking about, as if I didn't know?" she added dryly, following her cousin inside the fragrant kitchen.

"I can't help it," Mary Jo said. "I'm worried about you. With good reason, too. You haven't even opened that box of chocolate truffles I brought you!" She sobered. "You heard anything yet?"

"No, not from him or his lawyer," Eve replied tersely. She hated the limbo of uncertainty but could not bring herself to change it. Let Nate do the contacting, she thought angrily. She had to hold on to the anger. It sustained.

Her shrug concealed the anxiety that stalked her every breath. "But it's only been five days."

"Only, huh? To quote your favorite poet, 'Five years have passed; five summers, with the length of five long winters!'"

"Wordsworth did know how to say it," Eve replied with a thin laugh. "Coffee?"

"No, thanks. Why don't you call Nate?"

"Why should I call Nate? I told you what he said the night we parted. He left no doubt about what he means to do!" Subsiding, she sat down at the table. "Besides, he isn't due back from that convention until tonight."

"Then you'd better do *something*."

"I'm aware of that, Mary Jo!" She sighed. "I'm sorry, I didn't mean to snap at you. Look, we've already talked this subject to death, so let's get on to something else." A sparkle lighted her dull gaze. "Like your show next Tuesday. It's definite, M.J., I'll be there!"

"Well, Lord knows I'll need you," Mary Jo said soberly. She glanced outside at Amanda, still romping in the leaf pile. "When are you going to tell her about Nate?"

"When I think she should know."

"You're stalling, Eve," she chided gently. Eve's narrowing violet eyes quickened Mary Jo's voice. "Let me say just one more thing, then I'll hush. Nate loves you and you love him. And you both love that little girl out there." Rising, she urged, "Think about that, honey. And think with your heart, okay?"

"That's what started all this trouble in the first place, Mary Jo," Eve reminded with a bleak smile.

"I know. But Evie, wasn't it all worth it?"

"Yes, because of Amanda." Shrugging, Eve went on to something else.

Later that evening Hannah decided to go to a movie. Eve fixed supper, then installed Amanda in the den with her favorite cartoon video while she cleaned the kitchen. Outside, clouds blackened the sky and the house creaked in the wind. Eve shivered at the lonely sound. Nothing felt right anymore—her home, her routine, her empty, sterile bedroom. It was as if an entirely new person had returned to the little house on Willow

Lane. A person who didn't know how she really felt about anything.

Including the risk of putting her heart on the line again, she thought as Mary Jo's question resurfaced. *"But Evie, wasn't it all worth it?"* Viewed from that angle, had she been given the foresight that long-ago day, would she have chosen to set into motion the chain of events that had led to this desolate moment?

The answer came quickly and with searing honesty. She would live it all over again just to have been loved by Nathaniel Wright, even for a few fleeting hours.

It was staggering to realize how much she cared. The need to see him was a literal ache in both mind and body. Angrily she rejected it, along with the guilt nibbling at her defenses. She'd done nothing to deserve his condemnation. He'd been cruel and unjust, her stubborn pride reminded.

But so had she, Eve conceded cautiously. Accusing him of gross neglect of a child he didn't even know he had wasn't exactly fighting fair. He couldn't defend himself, she hadn't given him a chance. She'd lashed out at him, fulfilled her urge to retaliate, then run away. One by one, the protective shields fell away, allowing her to see with almost painful clarity the mistakes she'd made. She should have tried to talk it out, countered his charges in a calm, rational manner. Instead she'd allowed old hurts and resentments to guide her actions.

Anger vanished, leaving her appallingly vulnerable. Despite her valiant effort, tears blinded her as all her shattered dreams rose up to haunt her. She sank into a chair, covered her face with her hands and cried as if her heart would break.

When she was drained, she dried her tears, then went back to the den, where Amanda lay snuggled under her grandmother's afghan. Bracing her shoulders, Eve snapped off the television set and sat down beside the little girl.

"We'll turn it back on in a minute, love," she said, soothing Amanda's protests. "First, I have something to tell you. Something wonderful."

Drifting up from the dregs of slumber, Nate averted his eyes from the dull light coming through his windows. Groggily he wondered what time it was and why he didn't seem to care. Taking naps was not one of his habits, but he had worked insane hours every night this week, and fatigue had finally asserted its will.

Such dedication was not for the noble purpose of achievement, Nate admitted sardonically. The concise clarity of microchip technology was infinitely preferable to the murky haze that enshrouded his personal life. He'd talked to his attorney as soon as he'd arrived back in Portland. But he hadn't signed the papers that would begin legal proceedings for custody of Amanda. He would, though, he assured himself. Soon. He just wished there wasn't such a sense of finality to that act.

His gaze wandered back to the window. Mount Washington towered through a sullen drizzle, and birds huddled in the trees. They looked as miserable as he felt, he thought, rubbing his arms to warm himself. The rich mahogany-paneled walls of his study were softened by a velvety red carpet and the crackle of a fire. Yet the room felt cold and cheerless.

It was Saturday. He'd told Eve he'd see her Saturday. "You can count on that," he'd said.

Without warning, her image was everywhere—in his mind, his vision, his ravaged heart. *I miss her.* God, what an understatement. His belly twisted with it. He needed to be loved and held, to love and hold in return. That had a familiar ring to it, he thought with a grimace of humor. Was history repeating itself?

A sour grin eased Nate's mouth as Patrick sauntered in the open door. "I'm going to have to speak to Dusty," Nate growled. "Looks like he's letting just anything in these days. To what do I owe this dubious honor?"

"It's been a while, so I thought I'd better see how you were faring," Patrick replied breezily. "So how are you faring, friend Nate?"

Nate motioned to a chair. "Not worth a damn. How about yourself?"

"That about says it. You missed a good convention. Good time, too. You think you could rustle up a hot toddy? Chilly outside."

Nate rustled up one for himself while he was at it. Settling into comfortable chairs, the two men resumed their desultory conversation. At length, a moody silence fell between them. Nate got up to chuck another log on the fire.

"Seen Mary Jo lately?" he asked idly.

"No need to see Mary Jo. The lady made her wishes quite clear." Opaque blue eyes shifted to the Cézanne landscape hanging over the fireplace. "I am going to attend her show, though. Not as a buyer, however, since I've already bought three of her paintings. Anonymously, so keep that to yourself."

Nate frowned. "That's rather charitable of you, considering."

"I don't believe in charity," Patrick said shortly. "She's an investment and a good one." He ran a finger around his collar. "I'm also buying her Blazer."

"Why?" Nate asked irritably, beginning to pace. "It's obvious you want the woman, so why help her slip away?"

"Because I *wouldn't* have her. All I'd have is a dissatisfied female with a botched-up career. Anyway, the Blazer will come in handy on the farm." Tiring of the subject, Patrick picked up his briefcase and emptied its contents on Nate's desk. "Here's some literature from the convention, contacts I made there—"

"I'll look through it later. By the way, I've been thinking of opening a branch office in London early next year. Think you might be interested in heading it up?"

"You bet I would!" Patrick said. "Just say when."

"I thought after the holidays, but market-potential research could begin anytime. Deal?" he asked briskly.

"Deal!" Patrick said, and sealed it with a handshake.

There was a spring in Patrick's step. Watching him, Nate felt a minute lift of heart. He glanced at the clock. Two o'clock. He began pacing. *Eve*. Yearning sank its talons deep into his flesh as he pictured her lovely face and form, the bright sensual spirit she cloaked in wariness and caution. He'd loved seeing her happy....

Covertly Patrick scrutinized the man prowling the room like a caged tiger. "Dusty says you've been working like a maniac lately. Any reason for that?"

"Yeah, there's a reason." Nate sat down again. "I found out I'm a father, Patrick. Amanda's my daughter."

He whistled. "That's a reason, all right."

"You don't look all that surprised," Nate observed.

"Well, I am and I'm not. I did wonder, but it seemed so far-fetched, you know?" He cocked his curly black head. "You want to tell me about it, Nate?"

"Not particularly. But doubtless I will. You always did have a way of getting me to spill my guts," Nate drawled. Then, his voice dispassionate, he began talking.

When he finished, Patrick gave a judicious nod. "I can certainly see why you were so hard on her. That excuse about protecting Amanda is as flimsy as tissue paper. She should've been able to take one look at you and know what a fine upstanding man you are! No wonder you felt outraged. After a whole month together, still she said nothing. Why, you even proposed marriage to the woman! No doubt about it," he declared, "you had every right to tear into her like that."

Nate's eyes narrowed at his friend's fulsome defense. "I didn't exactly propose marriage, not in actual words—"

"Doesn't matter. She knew what you meant. And you had good cause to feel cheated, too," Patrick assured him.

"Dammit, I do have good cause! Amanda learned to walk, to talk, to become a *person* without me even knowing she existed!"

"Pure selfishness," came Patrick's ready agreement. "Eve could've found you if she'd really wanted to. Course, she did do a pretty good job of raising your kid alone, but still—"

"Oh, can it, Patrick," Nate advised gruffly. "We both know there was no way she could have found me. I also know a month isn't all that much time." He stopped, full of conflict because of what he sensed and what he knew. "I guess I thought love made a difference," he went on tiredly. Rousing himself, he added, "She has done a good job raising our daughter, though. A terrific job, in fact. But do you realize what knowing she lied does to me?"

"Of course. But I don't think she actually lied, Nate," Patrick said, abandoning his role of devil's advocate. "I think she just . . . didn't say."

"Maybe," Nate grunted, begrudging even that minor admission. Justified or not, anger and hurt still had a hammerlock on reason. He raked his hair in raw frustration. "Let's shelve it for now."

"All right. I've got to shove off, anyway." Patrick stood up and placed a hand on his friend's shoulder. "Nate, remember that night in the hospital when you said you needed an anchor? Well, you need one now, too. But I'm not that anchor any more. Eve is."

"How much longer, Mommy?" Amanda demanded for the dozenth time. "How long till we get to my daddy's house?"

"Not much longer, honey. According to the man at the gas station, we're practically there." Smiling at the eager face, Eve thought back to last night. Upon learning that Nate was her father, Amanda had erupted in a joyful babble of questions. Eve had answered as simply as possible. The enthralling tale of a daddy who was lost and now found fit right in with the little girl's love of fairy tales.

"Does my daddy know we're coming?" she asked.

"No. It's going to be a surprise," Eve replied gaily. She didn't feel nearly as happy as she sounded, but she was committed. Maybe the element of surprise will work with him, she thought quixotically.

"I'm glad Nate's my daddy," the excited little voice broke into her thoughts again. "I like him."

"I like him, too, baby. That's why I chose him to be your daddy," she replied softly.

"And he likes us."

"He loves us." Eve's confident voice concealed a nagging doubt. Nate loved Amanda but did he still love *her*? Would he be glad to see her? Or was this trip just an exercise in futility? "We'll soon find out," she murmured as they drew abreast of his mailbox.

Tall brick pillars supported elaborate wrought-iron gates scrolled with twin *W*'s. Spying a button set into a brass plate, she pressed it and identified herself to the disembodied male voice that paused as if startled, then bade her enter.

It wasn't Nate's voice. Whose? she wondered. Dusty's?

The gates opened. A gasp passed her lips as she drove through. The tree-lined arcade opened like a fan to reveal a Georgian house of old rose brick and crisp white trim set on a rolling expanse of parklike grounds. Meticulously trimmed shrubbery framed it. Stately old trees soared over the dove-gray roof, and down one side of a tawny lawn ran the delicious incongruity of an ancient stone fence nearly overrun by wild roses and honeysuckle.

Gazing at the long two-story structure, Eve felt daunted by its symbolic power and arrogance. The sweatshirt-and-jeans-clad Nate she knew seemed far removed from all this, and for a moment she wondered wildly what she was doing here.

The driveway circled beneath a covered portico. At least we won't have to run through the rain, she thought. Her breath came faster as she stopped the car and got out. Pink geraniums in white stone urns were spaced along the clean-lined veranda. Their commonality eased her trepidation somewhat.

"Is *this* my daddy's house?" came Amanda's tiny voice.

"Yes. This is your heritage, Amanda." *Something I could never give you, no matter how long and hard I worked.* "Amanda, wait!" she called, but the child was already out of the car and scampering up the steps.

The double doors swung open, and a grizzled, wiry man stepped out. Amanda froze. Eve caught up with her and smiled. "Hello. I'm Eve Sheridan. Are you Dusty?"

"That I am." Black button eyes crinkled. "And I reckon this is Amanda, cause Nate said she was prettier than a frog on a lily pad, and by golly, she is!"

Amanda giggled and readily took the hand he held out. Heels clicking on the parquet floor, Eve preceded him into the foyer. "Is Nate here?" she asked casually.

"No, he's not," Dusty answered with a faint smile. "He's en route to your house, Miss Sheridan."

"My house!" She flung a hand to her throat. "But why?"

"I can't rightly say. But don't fret, he's driving the Mercedes, and it has one of those fancy car telephones. You go on into the den, make yourself comfortable while I call him."

Mutely she did as he suggested. Amanda scooted past and headed for the blue-eyed cat lying like a stretch of gray velvet on the cream-puff carpet. She wasn't allergic to cats, so Eve let her pet the animal. Trying to calm her erratic heartbeat, she sat down on one of the luxurious red leather couches. Why had Nate gone to her house? Could it be for the same reason she'd come here? Despite caution's unflagging skepticism, her hopes soared.

Relaxing, she gazed around the beautifully appointed room, noting the oversize fireplace and its hand-painted tiles. Two tall, blue-gray porcelain sculptures of Siamese cats flanked the hearth. She didn't know Nate liked cats. Behind her, French doors opened onto a glass-enclosed lanai filled with flowers and plants. The rest of the wall was windowed, with a pleasing view of pool and cabanas, gardens and topiary, and beyond, a sweeping panorama of meadow and woods.

Books lay about and a varied selection of magazines graced the gleaming black coffee table. The ambiance was one of casual elegance. Just like Nate, she thought softly.

Amanda, tired of the cat, was busily checking out other fascinating items in the room. Eve ordered her to sit down before she broke something.

"Not to worry," Dusty said, returning with a silver coffee service and fine china accoutrements. "We've already child-proofed this room, got it all ready for her."

Eve's heart plummeted. Something inside her had refused to believe that Nate would really carry through on his threat. But the preparations he'd made seriously undermined that wistful illusion. Maybe she ought to leave! She half rose, then sank back down again. No, she wasn't going to run, not this time.

Dusty was still speaking. He'd reached Nate, who should be arriving within twenty minutes or so, since he'd doubtless be driving like a maniac.

Eve liked his crinkly eyed grin. "What did he say when you told him I was here?"

"Just that you were to stay here and wait for him. Tell you what, Amanda, I bet we can find some cookies and maybe even some toys if you help me look," he coaxed.

Eve nodded permission. She waited alone in the spacious room, sipping the coffee Dusty had brought. Her mind was buzzing, her body a tangle of nerves screaming with tension. It seemed an eternity before she heard a car approach.

The sound sent her flying to the mirrored wall of the bar. She'd dressed with painstaking care, lean red leather pants for allure, a shimmering black-and-white silk charmeuse blouse for chic, spike-heeled pumps for courage. Oh God, I match the furniture, she thought despairingly. Smoothing and tucking, she breathed in, out, long, deep.

Then Nate appeared in the doorway, and her mouth went as dry as dust.

In gripping silence, they stared at each other, warily, hungrily. Her pulses scrambled into double time as she caught the evocative scent of soap and after-shave. The smell of him, his husky voice and forceful maleness, flooded her senses. No other man had ever stirred her as he did. No other man ever would.

The look they exchanged dissolved their already crumbling walls. For him, too, she thought with a dizzying leap of heart. Or was she only seeing what she wanted to see? Her legs sagged with the weight of her hopes and fears. She leaned against the couch.

"You went to my house," she said at last.

"And you came to mine."

They shared a shaky laugh.

He came closer. "Because neither of us wanted the other to crawl."

"We both had a strong stand, solid reasons to back up our hurt and anger," she responded, joyous at even this thin line of communication.

"Yes. I'm sorry, Eve, sorry that I hurt you. I'll always regret that."

"I'm sorry, too." Eve swallowed over the lump in her throat. She was going to have to trust, and she might as well start now. "I love you, Nathaniel Wright. For as long as you want me, and even after, I will love you."

His mouth worked, but no words emerged. Couldn't he say it? Her face paled with a dread that seemed to char her very soul. The clock ticked off age-long seconds. Her heartbeat kept pace.

"Eve, my eternal Eve." Shaking free of rapture's paralysis, Nate came to her in a single stride. He cradled her face and gave her the fullness of his vulnerable, unguarded eyes. "I love you more than you'll ever know. Eve, when I told you that the first time, I was asking you to be my wife—" his mouth tilted ironically "—although it might not have sounded that way. Now I'm asking again. Marry me?"

"Yes, I'll marry you. Oh yes!" Eve kissed him wildly. Then, drawing back, she tackled the sole remaining shadow on her happiness. "But I do have a question. Did you ask before or after you realized Amanda was yours? Not that it's important, because I trust your love," she assured him. "I'd just like to know, that's all."

Nate replied promptly and with a profound sense of gratitude. "Before. But you're right, it isn't important. I want my daughter, oh yes, but even more do I want her mother. Amanda's become the light of my life. But you? You *are* my life." A little embarrassed at his poetic speech, he pulled her into his arms and buried his face in her perfumed hair. "God, I've missed you! All those years when I was searching for something to hold on to—or someone," he amended, recalling Patrick's parting words, "it was you. I didn't know it, but it was you." He vented a deep sigh. "I've been a fool, Eve. That, I do know."

"So have I, proud, willful . . ." The rest of her response was swallowed up in his fevered kiss.

As their lips met, the sweet agony of pain and need and love and hunger became a consuming fire that blazed with its own eternal flame. The very spark of life, Eve thought, lavishing him with love's radiant passion.

A rush of eager footsteps broke the kiss. With a muffled groan, Nate disengaged from Eve's clinging mouth and pliant body and turned to face his daughter.

She skidded to a halt in front of him. "Hi, Nate—" Her lashes dropped on a confused blush that wrenched his heart with its familiarity. "I mean, Daddy," she corrected herself. She looked at him as if asking him to share her delight. "Mommy says you're my daddy and this is my house!" she burst out again. "And Dusty says when it snows, Santa can park his sleigh and Rudolph on the roof and slide right down that big chimney!''

Her eyes held all the wonder in the world. Secretly Nate was amazed at how much he'd come to love her in this short time. Part of it was transferred affection, he supposed, for when he looked at Amanda, he saw a young, heartachingly innocent Eve.

"With no trouble at all, sweetheart," he said huskily. He knelt to her. "I'm very glad to be your daddy, for I love you very much. I hope you're glad, too."

"I'm glad. So's Mommy. She said of all the daddies in the world, she picked the bestest for me!"

"Well then, I guess you're one lucky little girl, because God also picked the bestest mommy for you," Nate said, his voice deepening as two tiny arms wound around his neck in total trust.

Standing with Amanda still in his arms, he looked at Eve. Her eyes seemed sprinkled with stars. A sense of grief and loss nearly overwhelmed him for an instant. That blasted fall! Had it not happened, he could have been with her at their baby's birth, and perhaps by now they could even have made another one together.

"You don't know how much I regret all those lost years," he said softly.

"Me, too, love," she murmured. "But it's over now, and tomorrow...."

"Tomorrow." Their gazes locked in intimate communion. Oblivious to everything but the message she was sending him, Nate returned it in full measure.

Regret whispered across his mind again. Then, turning away from the past, he held out a hand to his future, laughing exultantly as he swept her into a one-armed embrace.

"Daddy, can I have a pony?" Amanda demanded.

"I don't see why not," her father said.

"Oh, good Lord." Her mother groaned. "It's started already!"

* * * * *